FROZEN FARGO

Night was falling. Fargo had to get up. He had to keep moving. If he stayed there he'd freeze. His days of roaming the frontier wherever his whims took him would be done. He got his hands under him and pushed but his strength had deserted him. He rose only as high as his elbows and then fell back.

"Not like this, damn it."

Again, Fargo sought to rise. Again his body betrayed him. He lay staring up into an ocean of falling flakes, his consciousness swirling like the eddies in a whirlpool. He felt himself being sucked into a black abyss and there was nothing he could do to stop it.

Nothing at all . . .

THE TRAILSMAN

#332

BEARTOOTH INCIDENT

by
Jon Sharpe

A SIGNET BOOK

SIGNET
Published by New American Library, a division of
Penguin Group (USA) Inc., 375 Hudson Street,
New York, New York 10014, USA
Penguin Group (Canada), 90 Eglinton Avenue East, Suite 700, Toronto,
Ontario M4P 2Y3, Canada (a division of Pearson Penguin Canada Inc.)
Penguin Books Ltd., 80 Strand, London WC2R 0RL, England
Penguin Ireland, 25 St. Stephen's Green, Dublin 2,
Ireland (a division of Penguin Books Ltd.)
Penguin Group (Australia), 250 Camberwell Road, Camberwell, Victoria 3124,
Australia (a division of Pearson Australia Group Pty. Ltd.)
Penguin Books India Pvt. Ltd., 11 Community Centre, Panchsheel Park,
New Delhi - 110 017, India
Penguin Group (NZ), 67 Apollo Drive, Rosedale, North Shore 0632,
New Zealand (a division of Pearson New Zealand Ltd.)
Penguin Books (South Africa) (Pty.) Ltd., 24 Sturdee Avenue,
Rosebank, Johannesburg 2196, South Africa

Penguin Books Ltd., Registered Offices:
80 Strand, London WC2R 0RL, England

First published by Signet, an imprint of New American Library,
a division of Penguin Group (USA) Inc.

First Printing, June 2009
10 9 8 7 6 5 4 3 2 1

The first chapter of this book previously appeared in *Northwoods Nightmare*, the three
hundred thirty-first volume in this series.

PUBLISHER'S NOTE
This is a work of fiction. Names, characters, places, and incidents either are the product
of the author's imagination or are used fictitiously, and any resemblance to actual per-
sons, living or dead, business establishments, events, or locales is entirely coincidental.
    The publisher does not have any control over and does not assume any responsibil-
ity for author or third-party Web sites or their content.

If you purchased this book without a cover you should be aware that this book is stolen
property. It was reported as "unsold and destroyed" to the publisher and neither the
author nor the publisher has received any payment for this "stripped book."

The scanning, uploading, and distribution of this book via the Internet or via any other
means without the permission of the publisher is illegal and punishable by law. Please
purchase only authorized electronic editions, and do not participate in or encourage electronic piracy of copyrighted materials. Your support of the author's rights is appreciated.

The Trailsman

Beginnings . . . they bend the tree and they mark the man. Skye Fargo was born when he was eighteen. Terror was his midwife, vengeance his first cry. Killing spawned Skye Fargo, ruthless, cold-blooded murder. Out of the acrid smoke of gunpowder still hanging in the air, he rose, cried out a promise never forgotten.

The Trailsman they began to call him all across the West: searcher, scout, hunter, the man who could see where others only looked, his skills for hire but not his soul, the man who lived each day to the fullest, yet trailed each tomorrow. Skye Fargo, the Trailsman, the seeker who could take the wildness of a land and the wanting of a woman and make them his own.

1861, the Beartooth Range—where no one ever went because few had ever come back.

1

It was the worst blizzard Skye Fargo ever saw, and it was killing him.

Fargo was deep in the rugged Beartooth Range. Mountains so far from anywhere, few white men had ever visited them. He was there on behalf of the army.

"Scout around," Major Wilson had requested. "Let us know what the country is like. Keep on the lookout for Indian sign. And for God's sake, be careful."

It was known that the Blackfeet passed through the range now and then. So, too, did the Crows. Rumor had it another, smaller tribe lived far into the Beartooths, but no one knew anything about them. Like many tribes, they wanted nothing to do with the white man or his ways.

So far Fargo hadn't seen any Indians. He'd been exploring for six days when the first snow fell. It was just a few light flakes. Since snow in early September seldom amounted to much, he kept on exploring. The light flakes became heavy flakes—the kind that stuck and stayed if the temperature was right, the kind that piled up fast. Within two hours of the first flake falling, the snow was two feet deep and rising.

Fargo kept thinking it would stop. He was so sure of it, he went on riding even when a tiny voice in his mind warned him to seek shelter. A big man, he favored buckskins, a white hat and a red bandanna. In a holster on his right hip nestled a Colt. Under his right pant leg, snug in his boot, was an Arkansas toothpick in an ankle sheath. From the saddle scabbard jutted the stock of a Henry rifle.

A frontiersman, folks would call him. It showed in the bronzed cast of his features, in the hawkish gleam to his lake blue eyes, in the sinewy muscles that rippled under his buckskins. Here was a man as much a part of the wild land he liked to roam as any man could be. Here was a man who had never been tamed, never been broken.

The blizzard worried him, though. Fargo had a bedroll but no extra blankets and no buffalo robe, as he sometimes used in the winter. He hadn't brought a lot of food because he'd intended to fill his supper pot with whatever was handy.

Drawing rein, Fargo glared at the snow-filled sky. A deluge of snow, the flakes so thick there was barely a whisker's space between them, the heaviest snow he had ever seen, and that was saying a lot since he had seen a lot. He could see his breath, too, which meant the temperature was dropping, and if it fell far enough, he was in serious trouble.

"Damn," Fargo said out loud.

The Ovaro stamped a hoof. The stallion didn't like the snow, either. Great puffs of breath blew from its nostrils, and it shivered slightly.

Fargo shivered, too. Annoyed at himself, he gigged the Ovaro on.

As near as he could tell, he was high on a ridge littered with boulders. Humped white shapes hemmed him in. The game trail he had been following when the storm broke was getting harder to stick to. He hoped it would take him lower, into a valley where he could find a haven from the weather until the worst was over.

Shifting in the saddle, he gazed about. There were no landmarks of any kind. All there was was snow. Visibility six feet, if that.

Fargo's fingers were growing numb and he took to sticking one hand or the other under an arm to warm it. He tried not to think of his toes. He knew a fellow scout who had lost all the toes on one foot to frostbite, and now the man walked with an odd rolling gait but otherwise claimed he didn't miss his toes much.

Fargo would miss his. He was fond of his body parts and intended to keep them in one piece.

Since he couldn't see the sun, he had to rely on his inner clock for a sense of time. He reckoned it was about one in the afternoon but it could have been later. If the snow was still falling when night fell, he would be in desperate trouble. He tried not to think of that, either.

Fargo wasn't a worrier by nature. He didn't fret over what might be. He did what he had to, and if it didn't work out, so be it. Some people were different. They worried over every little thing. They worried over what they should wear, and what they should eat, and what they should say to people they met, and they worried over how much money they made, and whether they were gaining too much weight or going gray or a thousand and one other anxieties. They amused him no end. All the worry in the world never stopped a bad thing from happening.

But Fargo had cause to worry now. He would die if he didn't find somewhere to lie low until the worst was over. He would succumb to the cold, and his flesh would rot from his bones and a wandering Indian or white man would come on his skull and a few other bones and wonder who he had been and what he had been doing in the middle of nowhere and why he had died.

"Enough of that," Fargo scolded.

It helped to hear his own voice. To remind himself that he was alive and a man, able to solve any problem nature threw at him. He had never been short of confidence.

So on Fargo rode, looking, always looking for a spot to stop. An overhang would do. A stand of trees, even. A cave would be ideal but it had been his experience that life was sparing with its miracles.

More time passed. The only sound was the swish of the falling snow and the dull clomp of the Ovaro's heavy hooves.

The cold ate into Fargo. By now the snow was three feet deep in most places, with higher drifts. The drifts he avoided, if he could. They taxed the Ovaro too much, and he must spare the stallion.

Huge white shapes appeared. Boulders as big as log cabins.

Fargo had no choice but to ride between them. As he came out the other side, he nearly collided with a rider coming the other way. Instantly, he drew rein. So did the other man.

Squinting against the lash of snow, Fargo could make out the dark outline of the man and the horse, but nothing else. His hand on his Colt, he kneed the Ovaro alongside.

It was an Indian.

An old warrior—his hair nearly as white as the snow, his craggy face a testament to a life lived long and hard—studied Fargo as Fargo was studying him. He, too, wore buckskins, only his had beads on them. His mount was a pinto. It had black and white markings, like the Ovaro, only the patterns were different.

Fargo stared at the old warrior and the old warrior stared at him, and neither said anything. Fargo didn't see a weapon but no one, red or white, went anywhere unarmed.

The old man trembled. Not from fear, for there wasn't a trace of it on his face, but from the bitter cold.

Fargo looked closer and realized the old man was gaunt from hunger and haggard from near exhaustion. The eyes, though, were filled with a sort of peaceful vitality. They were wise eyes. Kind eyes.

"Do you speak the white tongue?"

4

The old warrior simply sat there, a shivering stature.

"I reckon not," Fargo said. Twisting, he fumbled with his cold fingers at a saddlebag and got it open. Rummaging inside, he found a small bundle of rabbit fur. Carefully opening it, he counted the pieces. He had six left. That was all. Without hesitation he took three out. He wrapped the rest and put the fur back in his saddlebag, then held out his hand to the old warrior.

"For you."

The old man didn't move.

"It's pemmican." Fargo motioned as if putting a piece in his mouth, and then exaggerated chewing. He held the pieces out again. "They're yours if you want them."

Caked with snow, flakes clinging to his hair and his seamed face, the old warrior stared at the pemmican and then at Fargo and then at the pemmican again. Slowly, as if wary of a trick, he extended his hand.

Fargo placed the pieces in the old man's palm. He asked who the old warrior was in Crow and then in the Blackfoot tongue and then the Sioux language, which he knew perhaps best of all Indian tongues from the time he had lived with the Sioux. He tried a smattering of other Indian languages he knew.

The old warrior just sat there.

Fargo resorted to sign language. Fingers flowing, he made the sign for "friend" and asked the man's name.

The old warrior never moved nor spoke.

"I don't blame you for not trusting me," Fargo told him. Not given how most whites treated Indians. "I'll be on my way, then." He didn't want to. The warrior might know where to find shelter from the storm.

Touching his hat brim, Fargo rode on. He didn't anticipate an arrow in the back, but he glanced over his shoulder to be safe and saw the old warrior staring after him. Then the snow closed in.

Fargo sighed. He had half a mind to turn around and follow the old man. He must know the mountains well. But it was plain the warrior didn't want anything to do with him.

Suddenly the Ovaro slipped. It recovered almost instantly and stopped.

Fargo leaned to one side and then the other, bending low to examine the ground. He couldn't be sure because of the snow but they appeared to be starting down a slope. The footing was bound to be treacherous and would become even more so if ice formed.

"Some days it doesn't pay to wake up," Fargo grumbled. He gigged the Ovaro.

The next hour was the worst. The snow never let up. Twice the Ovaro slipped, and each time Fargo feared he would hear the snap of a leg bone and a terrified squeal.

He was terribly cold. His skin was ice, and when he breathed, he would swear icicles formed in his lungs. His feet were numb, his hands slightly less so. He shivered a lot. His body temperature was dropping, and once it reached a certain point, he was as good as dead. There was a word for it, a word he couldn't recollect. But the word didn't matter. A person died no matter what the word was.

Fargo never thought he would end it like this. He'd always imagined going down with a bullet to his brain or his heart, or maybe an arrow or a lance. But not in the cold and the snow. Not by freezing to death.

The Ovaro slipped again, and this time it wasn't able to regain its balance. Fargo felt it buckle and he instinctively threw himself clear of the saddle. Or tried to. For in pushing off, he slipped on the snow-slick cantle and pitched headlong to the ground. He figured the snow would cushion his fall but he didn't land in snow; he came down hard on a snow-hidden boulder, his shoulder bearing the brunt, and pain shot clear through him.

The next moment he was tumbling and sliding.

Fargo envisioned sliding over a precipice and plummeting to his doom. He clawed at the ground but all he could grab were handfuls of snow.

A white mound loomed, another boulder, and he careened off it and hurtled lower.

Dazed and hurting, Fargo sought to focus. He thrust his hands into the snow but it had no effect. In fact, he was gaining speed, going faster every second.

Fargo swore. Sometimes a man did all he could and it wasn't enough. Some folks gave up at that point. What was the use? they figured. But Fargo never gave up. So long as he had breath in body, he fought to go on breathing.

Rolling onto his stomach, he jammed both arms and both legs into the snow.

It didn't work. The snow was too deep. No matter how hard he tried, he couldn't reach the ground. He couldn't find purchase. There was only snow and more snow.

Fargo had lost sight of the Ovaro. It could be lying above him with a broken leg. Or maybe it was sliding down the mountain, too. He vowed to go look for it. Provided he survived.

Another mound loomed. Frago threw himself to one side but the snow had other ideas. His other shoulder slammed hard. The pain was worse than the first time. Now both of his arms were numb. He had to struggle to move them even a little.

And he was still sliding.

His hat was gone, too. That made him mad. A hat was as necessary as footwear. It shielded a man from the heat of the sun and the wind-whipped dust and falling rain. He'd had that hat for a couple of years now, and he'd managed to keep it in fairly good shape.

Fargo peered ahead, seeking some sign he was near the bottom. He had the illusion he'd slid half a mile but it couldn't have been more than a few hundred feet.

Suddenly he shot off into space. He looked down but saw only snow. Flakes got into his eyes, and his vision blurred. He tried to twist so he wouldn't land on his head and neck, but he was only partway around when he smashed down with a bone-jarring impact. If he counted on the snow to cushion him, he was wrong. It felt like his chest caved in. He slid he knew not how many more feet and crashed against a boulder.

God, the pain! Fargo hurt all over. He thought half his bones must be broken. He marveled that he was still conscious, and tried to sit up. The attempt blacked him out. For how long, he couldn't say, but when the stinging lash of falling snow revived him, the sky was darker.

Night was falling.

Fargo had to get up. He had to keep moving. If he stayed there he would freeze. His days of wanderlust, of roaming the frontier wherever his whims took him, would be done. He got his hands under and pushed but his strength had deserted him. He rose only as high as his elbows and then fell back.

"Not like this, damn it."

Again Fargo sought to rise. Again his body betrayed him. He lay staring up into an ocean of falling flakes, his consciousness swirling like the eddies in a whirlpool. He felt himself being sucked into a black abyss and there was nothing he could do to stop it.

Nothing at all.

2

The cold woke him.

Fargo snapped awake, sucked out of the abyss by ice in his veins. Ice in his veins and in his flesh. Ice in his bones, in his marrow. He stared up into white. A white blanket of some kind. Confused, he tried to remember where he was and what had happened to him.

Without thinking, he opened his mouth and some of the white filled it. He coughed, and spat, and swallowed, and realized the white was snow, and then everything came back to him in a rush: the blizzard, being unhorsed, the slide, and the fall.

He was buried in snow.

Part of him wanted to stay there. Part of him wanted to lie there and let the cold seep through what little of him the cold hadn't reached, and to go over an inner precipice from which there was no turning back. But another part of him—the part that never gave up, the fighter—refused to go so meekly. That part of him struggled against the cold. That part of him fought with fierce intensity for his very life.

Somehow, the inner fight warmed him. Somehow, bit by bit he grew warmer, and bit by bit the cold faded until he felt almost himself again. The snow helped. The snow was a cocoon that once he was warm kept him warm.

Fargo tried to move his arms and found to his immense delight that he could. There was pain, but not more than he could bear. He moved them slowly at first, half afraid they were broken. They were fine. He wriggled his legs next, and tried his toes. His toes moved, but not as much as they should. He must do something about that soon, or he would come down with frostbite, if he hadn't already.

Fargo wanted to sit up but first he must do something about the snow. He thrust upward and it broke away, and clear, cold air rushed into his lungs even as bright sunlight nearly blinded him. Only a few flakes fell. The worst of the blizzard was past.

The sun was where it would be at about ten in the morning.

"I was out all night?" Fargo marveled. No wonder he had been so cold. It was a wonder he hadn't frozen.

Girding himself, Fargo slowly sat up. He pressed his hands to his ribs, to his hips, to his back. His body was intact. Bruised and battered and scraped, but intact.

Elated, Fargo made it to his feet. He swayed for a few seconds, in the grip of dizziness, but it went away. He breathed deep, relieved and grateful to be alive. He was even more grateful when he looked up and saw the cliff he had fallen over. It was sixty feet high, at least. The fall alone could have killed him. Fortunately, he'd landed in a deep drift, missing a cluster of boulders by only a few yards.

Damn, he was lucky. Fargo's elation, though, was short-lived. He gazed about him to find that he was at one end of a broad valley. Everything in it, and everything on the facing slopes, was buried in white. White, white everywhere, an unending vista of white and more white. And nowhere, not anywhere in that sea of white, did anything move.

Nowhere was there any sign of the Ovaro.

Fargo turned this way and that, searching, hoping against hope. He scoured the base of the cliff, fearful that the Ovaro had plunged over the cliff as he had done, but there was no other disturbance in the snow. Apparently the Ovaro was still up on the mountain.

Fargo craned his neck but couldn't see above the cliff. He had to get up there. He had to find the stallion and make sure it was all right. He waded forward, the snow as high as his thighs, but he took only a few steps when he received another unwelcome shock.

His Colt was gone.

Fargo turned and cast about where he had landed. He kicked snow aside. He dug with his hands. But if the Colt was there, he wouldn't find it until the snow melted. Or maybe, Fargo reflected, it was somewhere above the cliff. He slid far before going over the edge. Never once did he think to hold on to it so he wouldn't lose it.

"Damn me."

Fargo roved along the base of the cliff. He told himself there must be a way to the top, but if there was, he couldn't find it. The rock face was sheer, save for a few fissures, and they were too narrow to be climbed.

In a quarter of a mile, Fargo came to where the cliff ended. The slope beyond was deep with snow and so steep that when he started up, he took barely six steps before he slipped and fell and slid back down.

Only then, as Fargo stood and brushed himself off, did the full gravity of his situation hit him. He was stranded in the heart of the Rockies. He had no horse. He had no gun. He had no hat. He had no food or water. All he had were the buckskins on his back, and his Arkansas toothpick.

Or did he? The thought caused Fargo to squat and grope under his boot. He exhaled when he confirmed the knife was still snug in its ankle sheath.

"At least I didn't lose you." But now what to do? Fargo asked himself. He wanted to look for the Ovaro but he had to be practical. He needed shelter as well as something to eat. Once he was sure his toes were all right and he was warm and fed, he could strike out after the stallion.

Fargo gazed the length and breadth of the valley. Except

for where a few stands of trees had taken root, it was open. The trees, like everything else, were covered with snow, some so heavy with white, they were bent nearly to the ground. He made for the nearest stand. If he could find dry wood, he could get a fire going and warm his feet.

The glare blinded him. The sun was so bright that looking at the snow hurt his eyes. They kept watering. It got so bad, he kept his gaze down and his eyes narrowed to slits to spare them the misery.

His were the only tracks. For as far as he could see, the snow was unbroken. Not a living thing had been abroad since the blizzard ended.

A dry chuckle rattled from Fargo's throat. The animals had more sense than he did. They were snug in their burrows and dens. He would gladly trade places with any of them.

His boots made little noise. His toes had begun to hurt, and he hoped it wasn't a sign the frostbite had worsened.

The first stand proved to be mostly cottonwoods, which suggested water, but there was no spring. Fargo moved carefully among the pale trunks. He didn't find a single downed limb; they were buried under the snow. And since the branches on the bent trees were covered with wet snow, as well, his prospects of starting a fire were slim.

The next stand was almost a hundred yards away. Wishing he had his hat to ward off the sun, Fargo trudged toward it. He was thinking of his hat and not paying any attention to his surroundings, which was why he was all the more surprised when a low growl fell on his ears. He looked up. For a few seconds the glare prevented him from seeing anything.

Fargo blinked a few times. Suddenly everything came into sharp, stark focus. Including the two wolves studying him much as they might a deer or elk they contemplated devouring. He drew up short.

"Oh, hell."

Normally, wolves left humans alone. But these were lean

12

with hunger, their ribs showing through their fur. Their age might have something to do with it. There was gray in their coats and muzzles.

Sometimes the sound of a human voice scared wild animals off. Fargo tried it now. Waving his arms, he hollered, "Light a shuck, you four-legged idiots."

Both wolves turned and loped off, snow spraying from under their flying paws.

Fargo smiled. It worked. He started on again, and his smile changed to a frown.

The wolves had stopped. They were looking back at him. One growled. Then both came slinking toward him, their heads low, their teeth bared.

"Hell."

Fargo still had about fifty yards to go to reach the next stand. On flat, dry ground he might have stood a chance of reaching it before they got him. In the deep snow he stood no chance at all. Bending, he slid his fingers into his boot and palmed the Arkansas toothpick. Ordinarily it had a comforting feel. But a knife against two wolves? He was in trouble.

Fargo kept walking. He must get to that stand no matter what. In there he stood a prayer. He could put his back to a tree so only one wolf could get at him at a time. Out here they could attack from two directions at once. It would be easy for them to hamstring him and bring him down.

God, Fargo wished he had the Colt or the Henry.

The wolves had separated. They were coming at him from two sides, exactly as he predicted. They held their bodies low to the snow, their fur bristling. Both snarled and showed their teeth. Their eyes were fixed on him with the fierce intensity of starving animals.

Forty yards to go to the stand . . .

Fargo yelled at the wolves but all they did was take a few steps back and then resume stalking him. He resisted an impulse to run. All it would do was tire him out and make it easier for them.

Thirty yards to go, and now a wolf was a dozen feet out on either side of him. This close, their age was even more obvious. These two were at the point in their lupine lives when they would eat anything they could catch and bring down. And they were about to bring him down.

Raising both arms to make himself appear bigger, Fargo bellowed at one and then the other. Both crouched and growled but neither backed off. They weren't scared of him at all. They didn't care that he was human. To them, he was meat, nothing more.

Fargo hefted the toothpick. The doubled-edged blade was razor sharp. He could cut them, cut them deep. He would go for their eyes or their throats. Or their legs. They couldn't get at him if he crippled them.

Twenty yards to go and the wolves continued to pace him.

Fargo was beginning to think they wouldn't attack before he reached the trees. Suddenly the wolf on the right came at him in a rush, spraying snow. He spun toward it and the wolf on the left did the same. Neither came within reach. Both loped away but not as far back as before.

Fargo kept walking. They were testing him, taking his measure as they would a buck or a bull elk. He glanced from one to the other and back again, alert for sign of another rush.

Ten yards now, and Fargo would be in among the snow-laden trees.

The wolf on the right snarled and the wolf on the left answered, and in they came, as fast as they could, which wasn't as fast as they normally moved, but it was fast enough that they were both on him before he could break into a run to try to reach the stand.

Fargo slashed at the wolf on the right and it pranced out of reach. The wolf on the left nipped at his leg but he jerked aside. Its flashing fangs missed. He stabbed at its neck but he missed, too.

Both were growling. Hackles raised, they circled him.

Fargo twisted, trying to keep both in constant sight. His mind filled with images of them ripping into him and bringing him down, and he shook his head to dispel them.

The next moment the pair pounced, both at once, each going for a different leg. Fargo cut at one and then at the other. He barely drove them off in time. When they resumed circling they were closer.

Their next rush, they would have him.

Fargo knew it and they knew it. His mouth went dry. He broke out in a cold sweat. He must try something, but what? In anger he kicked snow at the wolf on the left and it skipped back a few feet. He kicked snow at the other one, and it did the same.

Instantly, Fargo hurtled toward the stand. The snow hampered him, clinging to his legs. He only managed a couple of steps when the wolves closed in again.

They weren't stupid, these wolves.

Fargo stopped and crouched. He held the toothpick out in front of him, pointing it at first one and then the other.

"Come and get me, you hairy sons of bitches."

The wolves growled and bared their fangs, their eyes glittering. And then they came at him again, and this time it was in earnest. They had gauged his reactions and his reflexes and they were ready to bring him down.

Fargo arced the gleaming blade at one and then the other. They ducked and dodged and snapped at his legs. He felt teeth rip his buckskins but his leg was spared. The one on the other side darted in. He cut at it to keep it at bay and the moment he turned away, the wolf that had ripped his buckskins was on him again. And this time its teeth found flesh.

Pain exploded like a keg of black powder. Fargo slashed, and his blade sliced deep. The wolf yipped and sprang back.

He whirled toward the other one just as it leaped. Its heavy body slammed into his chest, nearly knocking him down. He got hold of its throat and held it from him, the wolf snapping and clawing in a frenzy of starving need. He buried the toothpick once, twice, three times.

More pain, this time in his lower back. The other wolf had buried its fangs and was trying to brace its legs to wrench and tear him open. Fargo cut at its face and slit an eye. Howling, the wolf dashed out of reach.

The wolf he was holding bit at his arm and drew blood. Fargo had no choice but to shove it from him, and let go. It scrambled up and backed off, blood oozing from the stab wounds.

Both wolves resumed their slow circling. Bodies hunched, slavering and snarling, they were ferocity incarnate. The wolf with the cut eye dripped blood. The other wolf limped slightly.

Fargo was torn and bleeding and bitterly cold. The stand was so near—and yet so far. He must reach it or he would die. It was that simple. And he must do it before the blood he lost weakened him.

He must do it before he was helpless.

Firming his grip on the toothpick, Fargo risked all in a sudden spurt of speed.

The wolves rushed him.

3

Fargo sidestepped a vicious snap by the wolf on the left, and the wolf on the right immediately veered at his leg. Fargo slashed down, going for the eyes. The wolf jerked back and the blade sliced into the top of its head, eliciting a yelp.

Less than five yards to go.

Fargo pumped his legs, his breath coming in gasps as much from the cold as from the exertion. He was so close he could see a few leaves poking through the snow on the trees. Then a wolf slammed into his back, driving him to his knees. He twisted, and they were on him. Teeth found his wrist. His toothpick found a throat. A maw yawned at his neck and he sank the toothpick up under a furry jaw. His shoulder flared with torment, and he whirled. He stabbed, he cut, he thrust, he rent.

And then Fargo was down, on his belly in the snow, so spent he couldn't move, his body a welter of pain, his buckskins more red than brown. He waited for the bite that would end his life. But nothing happened. With a supreme effort he rolled onto his side and looked for the wolves and couldn't believe what he saw.

They were dead, the snow around them bright red, their necks and bodies punctured and cut, their fur a matted mix of gray and scarlet.

Fargo felt no elation. He felt weak and slightly dizzy and the cold was worse. Sluggishly, he got to his hands and knees. His leg was torn open. His wrist was bleeding. He lurched to his feet and staggered into the stand. He couldn't seem to walk right. He collided with a cottonwood and clumps of snow rained down, battering his head and shoulders. Exhausted, he slumped against the trunk.

This stand was the same as the first. No dry wood anywhere.

Fargo willed himself to stand and his legs to move. He needed a fire, needed a fire desperately. It would warm him, revive him, lend him the strength to patch himself together. He lurched through the stand to the far side.

In the distance was yet another stand. Or was it a strip of woodland that had crawled across the valley floor from an adjacent slope? He couldn't really tell for the glare.

Time was wasting. Whatever it was, Fargo trudged toward it. There had to be dry wood. There *had* to be. He realized he was still holding the toothpick, and that it was caked with blood and gore and bits of hair. He didn't care. He would clean it later. Right now the important thing—the *only* thing—was a fire.

"I need a fire."

His voice sounded strange. It was strained and raspy, as if someone else spoke. He swallowed and licked his lips.

"I need a fire."

That sounded better. Fargo lurched on. He snickered at how silly he was being. It wasn't like him. The thought stopped him in his tracks. His brow puckered. No, it wasn't like him. Something was wrong. The wounds and the loss of blood and the cold were affecting his mind. He plodded on, his teeth set, his shoulders hunched. He would make it there if it killed him.

The snow was terribly bright. Fargo worried about going snow-blind. Since there was nothing in front of him but snow, he closed his eyes and felt instant relief. He tried to think of something to take his mind off his plight. He thought of women he had known, and he had known a lot. Many he liked. Many more were willing partners in passion, and that was all. He tried to think of the one he liked the most, but in his dazed state all their faces blended into a confused jumble of warm smiles and hot lips.

There was one, once, though, a long time ago. She was special. He could remember her face but he couldn't recollect her name. That bothered him, and he couldn't say why.

Fargo opened his eyes. The woods appeared no closer than they had when he closed his eyes, so he closed them again and continued plodding. He had lost all feeling in his feet. His hands were numb. To warm his fingers he stuck them under his arms.

Fargo tried to whistle but his mouth was too dry. He decided to sing but couldn't remember the words to any of the saloon songs he must have heard a thousand times.

"What's the matter with me?"

A ridiculous question, Fargo told himself, since he already knew. It didn't stop him from plodding on. It didn't crush the flicker of hope. All he had to do was reach those trees and get a fire going.

"Is that all?" Fargo chuckled at his little jest. He was tired, so very tired. He wanted to lie down right there in the snow and fall asleep. But as weak and confused as he was, he knew that spelled certain death.

Fargo wondered why it was he couldn't think of that woman he had cared for more than all the others. Was that all females were to him? A tumble under the quilt? Granted, he had no interest in anything lasting. He wasn't out to get married. He had no hankering for a hearth and home. But still.

He opened his eyes. The woods were still far off. Too far, maybe. Could he reach them before he collapsed?

A shriek brought Fargo out of himself. It came from overhead. He blinked up into the glare and spied a hawk soaring on outstretched wings. A red-tailed hawk, over two feet from beak to tail. It shrieked again, as if frustrated that the snow prevented it from finding the mice and rabbits on which it loved to feast.

"I know how you feel."

The hawk banked and glided toward the mountains, rising until it was a mere speck.

"If I had wings I wouldn't be in this fix."

Fargo stopped and snorted.

"That was a downright stupid thing to say."

He took three more steps and his legs had enough. He fell to his knees, grinned at the distant woodland, and sank onto his side. The snow was warmer than it had been. It was as warm as a blanket. He closed his eyes and sank into it and drifted on tides of inner darkness.

It was buzzing that brought Fargo around. At first he thought it must be bugs. Flies, probably. Come to crawl on him now that he was too weak to stop them. He swatted at them and one of the flies grabbed his wrist. Another fly alighted on his cheek. He tried to brush it away and it buzzed at him. "I don't talk fly."

"What was that, mister?" a voice asked.

"He doesn't know what he's saying, Jayce," another voice said. "Look at him. He's half out of his wits."

Fargo opened his eyes. He had been out a good long while. The sun was low in the western sky. But it wasn't the sun that interested him. It was the boy and the girl hunkered at his side. The boy looked to be ten or thereabouts, the girl maybe twelve. They were bundled in clothes that had seen better days. Their gloves had holes in them. The boy wore a torn hat and the girl had an old scarf wrapped around her head and ears. Both had thin, oval faces, green eyes, and sandy hair.

"I take it I'm not dead," he croaked.

"Not yet, but you ought to be," the boy said. "I never saw so much blood. What on earth happened to you?"

"Wolves."

The boy stiffened and looked all around. "What wolves? There's two that's been trying to get at our chickens and sometime at us, and making our ma plumb mad."

"They're dead. Back a ways. Your ma can rest easy."

The girl put a hand to his brow. "I think you have a fever. And you're awful pale."

"How far to your ranch? If it's not far I can make it." Fargo tried to rise on an elbow but couldn't.

"We don't have a ranch, mister," the boy said.

"Your farm, then?"

The girl shook her head. "We don't have a farm, neither. I'm Nelly, by the way. Nelly Harper. This here is my brother, Jayce. Ma said we could go play in the snow and we saw you lying way out here. We thought you were a dead deer, and we could surely use the meat."

"We can't eat you, though," Jayce said, sounding vastly disappointed.

"You're welcome to come to our cabin if you want," Nelly offered. "It's warm there, and there's some soup left over."

Jayce glanced at her. "Ma might not like it. Maybe we should go ask her first."

"He's hurt," Nelly said. "Hurt bad. We can't just leave him lying there. Maybe Sten and his men will come."

"Hadn't thought of that." Jayce regarded Fargo while gnawing on his lower lip. "Say. Maybe he's one of them."

"I've never seen him with them before."

"So? He could be new." Jayce poked Fargo in the chest. "Tell us true, mister. Do you ride for Cud Sten?"

"Never heard of him," Fargo said. "Seems an odd name for a man to have," he added.

Nelly was chewing on her lip, too, but stopped. "Cud is short for Cudgel. They call him that on account of he likes to beat people with a club. His last name is Stenislaski or something like that but no one can ever say it right, so everyone just calls him Sten."

"You know a lot about him. Is he a friend of the family?"

"Gracious, no. Cud's a bad man, mister. A very bad man. He's killed folks and worse, Ma says. He keeps paying us visits even though she keeps telling him not to."

"Why doesn't your father run him off?"

Nelly grew sad. "In the first place, no one runs Cud Sten off. In the second place, we don't have a pa."

"He died," Jayce said, mirroring his sister's sorrow. "A bear got him. He was out chopping wood and a griz snuck up and ate him."

"I'm sorry," Fargo said to be polite. "Was this recent?"

"Oh, no," Nelly said. "About a year ago, it was. I miss him an awful lot. He was a fine pa."

"Yes," Jayce said, and his throat bobbed. Then, with a toss of his head, he stood. "I reckon sis is right and we should take you with us. Can you stand or do we have to help you?"

Fargo went to push to his feet and realized his hands were empty. He scooped at the snow near where his right hand had been when he passed out.

"What on earth are you doing, mister?"

"I lost something."

"Is this it?" Nelly asked, and her hand came from behind her dress holding the Arkansas toothpick by the tip.

"We didn't want you stabbing us," Jayce said.

"Hold on to it if you don't trust me," Fargo suggested. Just so he didn't lose it like he had lost everything else. He made it to his knees and then to his feet and swayed like a reed in a high wind.

"Are you dizzy?" Nelly asked.

"Some."

She stepped in close. "You can lean on me if you need to. Just be nice is all I ask. Some of Sten's men aren't so nice, and I don't like them very much."

Fargo took note of that. He took a step, and a second, and smiled, thinking he could do it on his own. But at the next stride his head went into a whirl, and it was all he could do stay upright. He put a hand on her shoulder and waited for the vertigo to pass.

"You're not doing so well, are you?"

"I've done better," Fargo admitted.

"You haven't told us who you are or what you're doing in these parts. It isn't often we get visitors."

"Except for Cud Sten," Jayce said.

Fargo remedied his lack of manners. But he didn't tell the complete truth. He left out the part about scouting for the army. "I like to explore new country, and the Beartooths are as new as country gets. I didn't think there was anyone living within a thousand miles of here."

"There's just us," Nelly told him.

Fargo took note of that, too. He had gained a little strength, and he started off again, leaning on her as lightly as he could and still stay on his feet. "What about the Indians?"

"What about them?" Jayce rejoined.

"Are you on friendly terms? There are a lot of hostiles in the mountains, and they've been known to lift white scalps now and then." Fargo regretted saying it the moment he did.

Both children got that fawn-in-the-glow-of-a-lantern look, and Jayce glanced anxiously up and down the valley as if afraid a war party was about to swoop down on them.

"We worry about Indians all the time. Pa used to say they'd leave us be if we left them be. And once he gave one of our cows to them."

"Now that he's gone," Nelly said, taking up the account, "Ma is afraid they might take us to live with them."

Fargo could see that happening. Now and then warriors took fancies to white women. "Why don't the three of you leave?"

Sister and brother looked at each other, and Nelly answered, "You'd best ask Ma. It's not up to us."

"I'd go if we could," Jayce said. "I'm tired of always having to be on the lookout for Sten and Indians and bears and whatnot."

Fargo was mildly surprised. Most boys his age would gladly live in the country rather than in a settlement or town. Boys thrived outdoors, running barefoot and fishing and hunting and catching frogs and snakes.

"I'd love to go through a day safe," Nelly chimed in. "I can't imagine what that's like."

"You make it sound awful bad here."

That was when Jayce, who was struggling in the deep snow, twisted his head around. "Say, mister, didn't you say you killed those two wolves?"

"As dead as dead can be," Fargo assured him.

"Then how come one of them is chasing us?"

4

Fargo stopped and half turned and a chill ran down his spine. One of the wolves was closing on them with surprising speed, given that its coat was spattered with red from the stab wounds he had inflicted. There was a grim intensity about its expression. Every dozen feet or so it staggered for a few steps, but then it came on again.

Fargo took the Arkansas toothpick from Nelly, who was staring at the wolf in terror. "Run."

Jayce faced the wolf and balled his fists. "We'll help you fight it off, mister."

"No," Fargo said. Stricken as it was, the wolf was still formidable. "Get to your cabin. Let your ma know."

Nelly had recovered from her shock enough to say, "It wouldn't be right to leave you. You're in no shape to do much."

"I don't want you hurt." Fargo gave her a push. "Either of you. Now *run*."

His tone spurred her into flying, and she pulled Jayce with her. But they took only a few steps and stopped.

"We can't."

It was all Fargo could do to stay on his feet. *"Run, damn it!"* he commanded, and this time they actually did. But they couldn't go very fast.

And the wolf was almost on them.

Fargo shook his head to try to clear it but it didn't help. He focused on the wolf and only the wolf. He would do what he could to delay it, but he wasn't going to fool himself. He didn't stand much of a chance. He hefted the toothpick and was appalled at how heavy it felt. It showed how weak he was.

The wolf came to a stop just out of reach, bared its fangs, and snarled.

Fargo would swear he saw hate in its eyes. Hate for the killing of its mate, maybe. Or maybe it was his imagination. "Come and get me." He hoped the children kept running. He didn't dare glance over his shoulder to find out.

Holding the toothpick low, he tried a feint, which the wolf ignored.

The movement brought on more dizziness. Worse, Fargo's gut churned, and bile rose in his throat. He went to swallow it back down, and thought, *Why bother?* He let it come all the way up—and out. He threw up on the wolf.

For a few moments the wolf was motionless.

Then it came at him so quick that Fargo couldn't get the toothpick up in time. Fangs tore into his shirt. Its weight drove him back. He tripped over his own feet and then he was on his back, holding the wolf by the throat while it snapped at his face and neck and growled in fury and sought to rip and rend with its claws.

Fargo summoned what strength he had left but it wasn't much. He couldn't hold the beast off him for long. Pain seared his side. Teeth gnashed an inch from his eyes. The wolf was practically beside itself; he looked into its eyes and saw hellfire.

Fargo tried to roll so that he could pin it with his body but he couldn't do more than raise a shoulder. Again the fangs snapped, missing his neck by a whisker. He locked his elbows to keep it from reaching him but his arms were forced lower. His end was near. He sensed it, and the wolf sensed it. In a surge of ferocity, the wolf bit at his jugular. He twisted his neck away but he was only delaying the inevitable.

The next moment Fargo's strength gave out completely. The wolf's face filled his vision. Teeth were everywhere. He braced for a final explosion of pain, but there was an explosion of a different kind. Thunder boomed, and the wolf jerked to the impact of a heavy slug. It looked up, and thunder boomed again. Blood and hair and bits of an eyeball sprayed over Fargo's face, and the wolf went limp.

He couldn't hold it up. He felt his arms start to give out.

The world went dark.

"Can you hear me?"

Fargo was conscious of a warm hand on his forehead. He opened his eyes and could barely see for the glare. "Who . . . ?"

"I'm Mary Harper. You're in a bad way. I sent Nelly and Jayce to fetch our sled. But it will take them a bit."

"Sled?" Fargo said in confusion. His mind was a jumble. He could hardly think.

"To haul you to our cabin. You're too heavy for us to carry. And I wouldn't want to try, the shape you're in."

"Can't see," Fargo said. He swallowed and blinked, and there she was, her face as close as the wolf's had been. She was a vision: blond hair that glowed like a halo and the most incredible green eyes and small, full lips. There was no wariness in her eyes, only concern. "You're beautiful," he said before he could stop himself.

Mary Harper smiled. "You're not in your right mind. You've lost a terrible amount of blood."

"Sorry."

"For what?"

"Being so helpless," Fargo replied. It embarrassed him. Yet he had to admit it was a strange thing to be embarrassed about.

"It's not as if you planned it."

"Lost horse," Fargo tried to explained. "Fell off mountain. . . . so much snow . . . couldn't stop."

27

"Hush. Don't waste yourself. You can tell me all about it later, after we have you warm and bandaged and fed."

"Don't want . . . to be a burden."

"There you go again," Mary Harper said, kindly. "Please. Don't think anything of it. I would do the same for anyone in the shape you are. Indians included."

Fargo believed she would. An awkward silence fell—awkward to him, at any rate—and he said to fill it, "Can't believe you're here."

"My children were gone too long and I came looking for them."

"No. I mean, I can't believe you're *here*." Fargo tried to motion to encompass the valley and the mountains but couldn't move his arm far enough.

"Oh. To tell you the truth, there are days when I can't believe it, either. When I wonder what I was thinking when I let my Frank talk me into it. But, God, I loved that man."

"I heard about the griz."

Mary's features clouded. "The bear comes back from time to time. I shot at it once but don't think I hit it. Mark my words, though. I'll make it pay for what it did to my Frank."

Fargo had more he wanted to say, but a great weariness came over him and he closed his eyes and was out. Movement brought him around. He was being jostled, but gently.

"Careful now, Jayce. Don't drop him."

"I won't, Ma."

"Nelly, lift his legs higher if you can."

"I'm trying. He's so big, Ma. Bigger than Pa."

"There. That should do it. Now, Nelly, you spread the blanket, and all three of us will pull."

Fargo was on his back, a hard surface under him, his arms folded across his chest. He felt himself being covered. Blinking, he tried to raise his head.

"Lie still," Mary said. "We just got you on the sled. It will be a while before we get you to the cabin."

Two ropes had been tied to the runners, high up at the front. Mary took hold of one and her children took hold of the other. Bent at the waist, the ropes across their shoulders, they put their whole bodies into it. The sled moved a few inches, and stopped.

"It's hard, Ma," Jayce said.

"I know. But if we don't get him to our cabin, he'll die, son. Let's try again."

The sled jerked forward, stopped, and jerked again. This time it kept going. The crunch of the runners through the snow and the heavy breathing of the three pulling the sled soon lulled Fargo into limbo. He didn't fight it. He was so weak from blood loss, he didn't have the energy.

When Fargo woke up they were still huffing and puffing and the sled was still crunching. But instead of blue sky above him, there were tree branches. They were in the woods. He licked his lips and got an elbow under him so he could try to sit up.

"Don't even think it," Mary Harper warned. To her children she said, "Let's stop and rest again."

"Fine by me, Ma," Jayce said. "My shoulder is about rubbed raw."

"With me it's my hands," Nelly said. "My blisters have blisters."

"We're almost there. Another few minutes."

Fargo said, "If you'll help me up, I'll try to walk."

"Nothing doing," Mary responded. "You wouldn't make it, and we'd have to go to all the trouble of putting you back on the sled."

Her face floated above him. She placed her palm to his brow, probed for a pulse in his wrist, and scowled.

"What is it, Ma?" Jayce asked.

"Nothing."

"You're fibbing. And you always told us not to ever fib. Is he dying, Ma? Is that it?"

29

Mary Harper looked sadly down at Fargo and didn't say anything. Her expression was more eloquent than words could be.

Fargo forced a chuckle. "I'm that bad off, am I?"

"Do you want the truth?"

"Nothing but."

Mary's throat bobbed, and she touched the back of her hand to his cheek in a gesture of sympathy. "I'm no doctor. Oh, I can set broken bones and sew up cuts, and I have a few herbs for croup and the like. But you need a sawbones. Without one, without a hospital where they can tend you proper, well . . ." She bit her lip. "I can't offer any guarantees."

"I wasn't expecting any." Fargo softened his tone. "Look, we hardly know each other. But something tells me you'll do the best you can. I'm in as good a pair of hands as any."

She looked at him strangely, then gazed off into the trees, her face in profile as lovely as any he ever beheld. "It's not far. Once I dress the bites and get some soup into you and we put you to bed, the rest will be in God's hands." She patted his shoulder. "If I were you, I'd do a lot of praying."

"I'm not much for bending my knees," Fargo confessed.

"Then we'll pray for you. Never underestimate the power of the Almighty, Mr. Fargo. The Good Lord has kept my children and me alive."

"But not your husband."

Mary glanced sharply down. "No, not my Frank. And if I live to be hundred, I'll never understand why God saw fit to take him. The kindest, most decent man I ever knew. Why, Mr. Fargo? Why do bad things happen to good people?"

"Hell. You're asking the wrong man. Find yourself a parson. I gave up looking for answers long ago."

"I'm sorry to hear that, Mr. Fargo. A person needs to have faith in this life. Without it, what else is there?"

Fargo figured she really didn't expect an answer. He wearily closed his eyes and immediately dozed off. A jolt brought him back to the world of the living. That, and a loud thump.

"At last!"

"Nelly, you heat up water. Jayce, bring in extra firewood."

Fingers pried at Fargo's buckskins. The dry blood had caked them to his skin and they wouldn't come off. There was a tug, and then fingernails peeled at his shirt.

"I'm afraid I'll need to cut these off."

More reason for Fargo to miss the Ovaro. He had a spare shirt in his saddlebags. "Do what you have to."

As she worked, he faded in and out of consciousness. The warm cloth she used to wash the blood off felt wonderful. She used a needle and thread to stitch the bites and claw marks, and that didn't feel wonderful at all. Each time the tip of the needle pierced his skin, he gritted his teeth.

"Sorry if I'm hurting you," Mary said.

Fargo passed out again. When next he looked around, he was in a bed with blankets pulled to his chin. He did not need to pull them down to know he was naked. He brought an arm out from under and laid it on top.

The bed and a dresser were the only furniture. A single candle on the dresser cast flickering light.

A door opened, and in came Mary, carrying a wooden tray. On it were a steaming bowl of soup, a spoon, and a thick slice of buttered bread. She set the tray on the edge of the bed and sat next to him.

"Oh. You're awake. Good. It saves me having to wake you to get some food into you."

Fargo's mouth watered. His stomach growled louder than the wolves had. "That sure smells good."

Once again Mary Harper felt his forehead. "You're burning up. I don't have a thermometer, but I'd guess your temperature to be at least one hundred and three."

"I'm more interested in that soup." Fargo attempted to sit up, but once more his body betrayed him.

"Let me." Mary dipped the spoon and brought it to his lips and carefully let the broth trickle into his mouth.

Fargo had never tasted anything so delicious. He yearned to grab the bowl and down the soup in great gulps, but fortunately he was too weak. And it might make him sick.

Mary took her time. Whenever any got on his chin, she wiped it with a cloth.

Warmth spread from Fargo's belly. It made him drowsy, and the last thing he wanted was to pass out again. To try to stay awake he remarked, "You make the best chicken soup ever."

"Thank the chicken. And Nelly. She plucked it." Mary's mouth tweaked down. "We have seven left now."

"You killed one of your chickens just for me?"

Before she could answer, Jayce rushed breathless into the bedroom. He had been outside and was bundled in his threadbare coat. "Ma! Ma!"

"Calm down, son. You're acting as if it's the end of the world."

"A rider is coming. I was out chopping firewood and saw him."

Mary stiffened. "Just one? Do you know who it is?"

"Yes, ma'am. It's one of Cud's men. That mean killer. The one they call Tull."

5

There wasn't much space under the bed. Barely enough for Fargo to keep from scraping his nose on the slat when he turned his head. Through the closed bedroom door came muffled voices and the patter of feet on the floorboards. He gathered that Mary and the kids were scurrying about, cleaning and hiding any trace he was there.

Mary had insisted he get under the bed. "It's for your own good. I can't predict what Tull will do if he finds you."

"Give me a gun and I'll take my chances."

"All I have is a rifle, and in the shape you're in, you wouldn't be much use with it."

The hell of it was, she was right.

Fargo could tell all three were scared. Nelly, especially. The girl had become as pale as a ghost. Suddenly the bedroom door opened and there she was, practically shaking with fear.

"Ma says to tell you he's almost here. She says not to make a sound. And whatever you do, don't come out from under there."

Fargo grunted.

"You might want to scoot back against the wall. If he comes in here, he'll see you."

"Don't worry about me."

"I can't help it. I like you." Nelly's thin mouth quirked in a nervous smile, and she closed the door behind her.

The scooting took some doing. By levering his elbows

33

and wriggling, Fargo was able to slide far enough back that unless Tull got down on his hands and knees, he should be safe. It rankled him, though, this hiding. He had never hidden from trouble in his life.

The cabin grew quiet. Outside, a horse whinnied, and soon Fargo heard the low, gruff voice of the rider. Spurs jangled, and there was talk, Mary's and the man's, mostly, the man's rising in anger. It was hard to tell what they were saying, though. Then, without warning, the bedroom door was flung wide.

Scuffed boots with large spurs entered and stopped midway. The boots turned from side to side.

Mary's shoes appeared behind them in the doorway. "I can't say I like you barging in here like this, Mr. Tull. A gentlemen wouldn't behave as you do."

"Who the hell is a gentleman?"

Fargo disliked the man, sight unseen.

"As you can see, no one is here. I told you there's just me and the children. Why didn't you take my word for it?"

"I'm not Cud, lady. You don't mean bear squat to me."

"Has anyone ever mentioned how crude you are?"

"Don't put on airs." Tull's boots moved to the closet, and the closet door opened. "I saw tracks on my way in. Boots tracks. And I found two dead wolves. They hadn't been dead all that long."

"It has nothing to do with us."

"So you say. But right where the boot tracks end, sled tracks begin. And the sled tracks come right to your cabin."

"The children were out sledding after it snowed. The tracks you saw must be Jayce's."

"His feet ain't that big."

"I've seen tracks get bigger when snow starts to melt."

Tull gave a snort. "You must think I'm as dumb as a stump. It hasn't warmed up a lick since the blizzard."

Fargo heard clothes rustle.

"See? No one is in there. Now why don't I fix you some coffee and you can tell me why you're here?"

The boots turned and took a step toward the bed. Fargo tensed, firming his grip on the toothpick. But the boots stopped a few feet away, and Tull didn't bend down to look under the bed.

"Cud sent me ahead to make sure you and the brats are all right. He's still a few days out and couldn't come fast on account of the cows."

"Cows?" Mare repeated.

"Oh, hell," Tull declared. "Now he'll be mad at me. I wasn't supposed to give it away."

"Why would he be bringing cows? I can't afford to buy them. I have no money. He knows that."

"We rustled a herd a month ago and he kept six out just for you. As a present." Tull swore. "About makes me sick how he carries on about you. Used to be, Cud Sten was the hardest man I knew. Then he met you and went all to hell."

"I'll thank you to watch your language around the children."

"I'm not changing how I talk for you or anyone else. And don't think crying to Cud will help. I'm not scared of him like some of the others are."

"He's a very dangerous man."

"*I'm* a dangerous man," Tull said matter-of-factly. "In case you ain't heard, I've put windows in the skulls of more men than Cud and all the rest put together, including that damn sneaky Rika."

"You're a natural-born killer. I'll grant you that," Mary Harper said. "Which is why I want you on your way as soon as possible. I won't have you around my children any more than can be helped."

"You have your gall. Just because you're female, don't think you can insult me and get away with it. And who says I'm going anywhere?"

"What?"

"Cud wants me to stay until he gets here. To watch over you, as he put it." Tull's laugh was ice and spite. "You and me can get better acquainted."

"Lay a hand on me and I'll gut you. So help me, I will."

"Damn, you think highly of yourself. But don't worry, lady. If I can't pay for it, I don't bother with it."

"What is he talking about, Ma?" Jayce asked.

"Nothing, boy," Tull said, and laughed. "You sure got some innocents, don't you?"

"Leave them out of this."

"Sure, lady. Sure. How about that coffee? I about froze riding here."

Fargo took a risk. He moved his head enough to peer out.

The man called Tull was almost to the doorway. Of middling height and build, he wore a brown hat and cowhide vest. The hair that poked out from under the brown hat was black. On his right hip, in contrast to his rumpled clothes, gleamed the pearl grips of a nickel-plated Colt. He half turned in the doorway, revealing a lean face stamped with cruelty.

Fargo drew back before he was spotted.

Tull's boots moved into the next room. He left the door open.

Now Fargo could hear what was being said. And from where he lay, he could also see a small part of the main room, including part of a table and a couple of oak chairs.

Tull took a seat, his back to the bedroom. "Hurry with that coffee, damn it. I need to warm my innards."

"Please, Mr. Tull," Mary said, bringing over a steaming cup with a saucer under it. "I keep asking you." She walked off.

Tull took the cup and drained it in a few gulps. "Ahhh. That's nice. Real nice. Give me another." He shifted and stared at something Fargo couldn't see. "What are you two looking at?"

"Nothing, sir," Jayce said.

"Then quit staring."

"We don't get many visitors. Even your kind."

"What the hell does that mean? Never mind. I think I know. That's your ma talking." Tull poked a thick finger in their direction. "I won't warn you again. I don't cotton to being stared at. Never have."

Mary came back, carrying the coffeepot. "Since you insist on staying, you can at least be civil."

"You're a trial, lady. If you weren't Cud's woman, I'd get more riled than I am."

"Where do you intend to sleep while you're here?"

Tull stomped the floor with his left boot. "Right here will do. I've got my own bedroll, so I won't put you out any."

About to pour, Mary paused. "I won't have you under the same roof with my children and myself. It's not proper."

Tull laughed. "What you want doesn't count. It's what Cud wants. And what Cud wants is for me to keep an eye on you until he gets here, proper or not proper."

"Where am I going to go in the dead of winter with no horse and two children to look after?"

"It's not that. It's the Injuns. We struck redskin sign, and he's worried they might pay you a visit."

"They haven't bothered us since my husband gave them one of our cows. Why would they harm us now?"

Tull shrugged, then waggled his empty cup. "Don't ask me. I wouldn't care if they helped themselves to that pretty hair of yours. I just do what Cud tells me. And since he said I stay, I stay. Now give me some more coffee, damn it." Nelly moved between Fargo and the table. She was watching her mother and the outlaw and didn't realize she was blocking Fargo's view. He moved so he could see past her.

"What if I were to insist that you leave?" Mary was saying. "I'll tell Cud it was my doing so he won't be mad at you."

"Don't your ears work? I don't do what you say. I do what Cud says. I'm here and I am staying. The sooner you accept that, the sooner you'll stop annoying me."

Mary carried the pot out of Fargo's sight. When she came back, she was holding a large towel over both of her hands. "What if I ask you to leave as a personal favor to me?"

"God Almighty," Tull declared in disgust. "You'd make a great dog. You worry every bone."

" I'm a woman without a husband, and it wouldn't do for me to have the likes of you staying under my roof. In a town it would create a scandal."

"But we're not *in* a town," Tull said in rising exasperation. He cocked his head and gave her an intent scrutiny. "What are you up to?"

"I beg your pardon?"

"You've been acting peculiar since I rode up. Now you practically want to throw me back out." Tull scratched the stubble on his chin. "It makes me think you're up to something."

"Don't be silly."

Tull ignored her. "I keep thinking of those boot tracks. And the sled sign. Where is he, woman?"

"Where is who? You've already searched the whole cabin and didn't find anyone."

"I think I'll search again." Tull rose and hooked a thumb in his belt near the pearl-handled Colt. "Only this time I'll search in every little nook and cranny."

Fargo drew back. He was in no shape to go up against a man like Tull. If he had his Colt, it would be different. It didn't take a lot of strength to thumb back a hammer or squeeze a trigger.

"I resent this," Mary said indignantly.

"Do I look like I give a damn? How about if I start with the fireplace."

"Ma?" Nelly said.

"Hush."

Tull's boots moved out of sight and Fargo heard a metallic clang. A fireplace poker, he guessed. There were other sounds, thuds and scrapes, and then Tull exclaimed, "Well, what do we have here? Looks to me to be a bloody towel you tried to bury under these ashes."

"That old thing?" Mary said, stepping into view. "I stuck it in there days ago. I cut my finger peeling potatoes."

"There's an awful lot of blood. Are you sure you didn't cut off your whole hand?"

"You're not funny."

"I think I am. And lookee here. You say you cut yourself days ago? But when I picked up this towel, I got some of the blood on me." Tull chuckled. "Here, girl. Catch."

"Don't do that!" Nelly cried, and dashed to her mother, who took her into her arms.

"That was uncalled for, Mr. Tull. I won't have you scaring my children," Mary said.

"Hell. Can't any of you take a joke?"

Footsteps and jingling spurs came toward the bedroom. Tull stopped just inside and Fargo imagined him looking around.

"You checked in there," Mary said.

"Did I?" Tull moved to the closet, opened it again, and squatted. He picked up a pair of shoes with holes in them. "Don't you ever get tired of being so god-awful poor?"

"We get by."

"You should stop saying no to Cud. He'd see that you got dresses and shoes and whatever else females cotton to."

"I can't be had for money or clothes. Or anything else."

"Oh? How did your husband hook you, then?"

"With love."

Tull uttered a short bark. "Love? It's nothing but a fancy word that those like you use so you won't feel guilty about letting a man undo your petticoats."

"I was wrong about you, Mr. Tull. You're not just crude. You're despicable."

"Another fancy word. All it means is that you think you're too good for the likes of me."

Fargo saw Tull's boots swivel toward the bed.

"Are you done in here?"

"Not yet. There's one place I forgot to look the first time. Probably because I figured no one would be stupid enough to hide there."

The scuffed boots approached, but not too close. A gun hammer clicked, and the man called Tull said, "How about if I shoot this bed a few times and we see if anything pops out?"

6

The bed wouldn't stop the slugs. They would pass all the way through, and into Fargo. He was debating whether to crawl out meekly when Mary Harper intervened.

"Please don't. He's under there but is badly hurt. He can hardly move."

"The truth at last." Tull took a few steps back. "You got a weapon under there with you, mister?"

"No," Fargo answered. He placed the toothpick against the wall, where it was darkest.

"Do you expect me to believe that? Let me see both your hands, and they damn well better be empty."

Fargo complied.

"That's good. Now crawl on out of there, nice and slow."

"I couldn't do it any other way." Fargo gripped the edge of the bed and pulled, but he was so weak he hardly moved. He tried again with no better success.

"I don't have all day."

Mary said, "I told you. He's hurt. You saw the dead wolves. You saw all the blood. We brought him here and put him to bed, and I was just starting to feed him when you came."

"Then you and the brats help him out. Any tricks, and I shoot your girl and boy."

"We'll do whatever you say," Mary assured him. "Just go easy on that trigger."

Hands reached under and gently dragged Fargo out. He

did his best to help. Tull stayed well back, his pearl-handled Colt steady in his head.

"What's your handle, mister?"

Fargo told him.

"Looks as if those wolves about ripped you to pieces. Get up in that bed while I ponder what to do with you."

Mary and the children helped. Without them, Fargo couldn't have made it. He sank wearily onto his back and clenched his fists in frustration. He had never felt so damn helpless.

"Move away from him," Tull commanded the Harpers. He came over, the Colt's muzzle fixed on Fargo's head. He looked Fargo up and down, then held out his other hand, palm open. "Push on this."

"What?" Fargo said.

"You heard me. Push my hand as hard as you can. Don't hold back, neither. I'll be able to tell."

Again Fargo had to do as the man wanted. He used his left hand, and he exerted all the strength he had, grimacing from the pain it caused.

"That's enough," Tull said. "She was telling the truth. You're as weak as a kitten." He bent and peered under the bed.

Fargo had a few anxious seconds until the outlaw straightened.

"I don't see no pistol or rifle under there. What happened to your hardware?"

Since there was no reason not to tell the truth, Fargo did, keeping his account short and to the point.

Tull chuckled. "All that, and now me. This ain't your day, is it?" He pursed his lips. "Or maybe it is. You get to live, for now. Give me any trouble, and I will buck you out in gore."

Mary said, "Thank you, Mr. Tull."

"Hell, lady, I'm doing this only because Cud might want to have a few words with this gent before he kills him. And besides, he's so puny he couldn't hurt a fly." Tull gestured at the doorway. "Out you go, all three of you." He backed after them.

"Stay in that bed, mister, you hear?" He started to turn.

Fargo's stomach growled, prompting him to say, "I can use something to eat."

"Eh?"

"I'm half starved. I'd be obliged if you'd let Mrs. Harper finish feeding me."

"Would you, now?" Tull chuckled. "Why waste good food on a dead man?" He shut the door and his spurs jangled.

Fargo hadn't counted on this. He figured that with some food in him, he'd be able to crawl under the bed, get the toothpick, and have a nasty surprise for Tull the next time he came in.

"Now what?" Fargo wondered out loud. The longer he lay there without a bite to eat, the weaker he would get. He remembered Tull saying it would be three days before Cud Sten showed up. By then he would be so weak, he wouldn't be able to lift a finger to save himself. There was only one thing to do. But could he, in his condition?

Fargo doubted Tull would come back in anytime soon. He should have all the time he needed. Placing his hand over the side of the bed, he slid toward the edge. It took all he had. His wounds weren't to blame so much as all the blood he had lost. If he hadn't lost it . . . He gave his head an angry toss. A long time ago life had taught him that ifs were so much thin air. Ifs were make-believe. What mattered was what *was*.

With an effort, Fargo eased his shoulder over the edge. He was careful to go slow—not that he could go much faster if he wanted to—and when gravity took over, he got his arm under him to cushion the short drop. He surprised himself. He made it without adding to his agony. After resting a minute, he crawled under the bed and extended his hand as far as he could reach. It wasn't quite far enough. He crawled a little farther and his fingers closed on the toothpick's hilt.

Getting out of bed had proven easy enough but getting back in wasn't. Twice Fargo tried to rise, and twice he sank back, betrayed by his own body. He considered staying on the floor. That might make Tull suspicious and he needed Tull close to use the knife.

Putting both forearms on the bed, Fargo gritted his teeth and marshaled his muscles. He couldn't get all of himself up, but he did succeed in sliding his shoulders and the top of his chest onto the sheets. After another break, he managed the rest of him. It left him exhausted and caked in sweat.

Fargo curled on his side with his back to the door, the toothpick low against his leg. "Puny, am I?" he muttered. "I'll show you, you son of a bitch." He closed his eyes, thinking to rest a bit, and was startled when he opened them again to find the room plunged in darkness. The candle had gone out, or someone had blown it out.

Fargo rolled over. The cabin was quiet. He glanced at the bottom of the bedroom door. No light showed. He reckoned night had fallen, and the others must have turned in. Tull, too, evidently.

The sleep had done Fargo some good. He felt a little better, except for a dull ache in the pit of his stomach. He was so hungry his mouth watered at the thought of food.

Ever so slowly, Fargo slid his legs over and placed both feet flat on the floor. The boards were cool on his naked soles. All he had on were his pants, courtesy of Mary before she hid him under the bed. He admired that lady, admired her a lot. She had a sharp head on her shapely shoulders. And she had uncommon courage. He couldn't imagine what it must be like for her, stranded deep in the Beartooth Mountains, living on the razor's edge of existence, the lives of her children hanging on her every decision.

Fargo tried to stand. He willed his legs to raise him and

they got him halfway up. Then they gave out and he plopped back down. This wouldn't do. It wouldn't do at all. He concentrated all his will and this time his legs did as he wanted but when he was all the way up a bout of light-headedness nearly brought him down again. He swayed but steadied himself.

The door, a vague outline in the dark, seemed impossibly far away. He shuffled toward it, sliding first one foot a few inches and then the other. His stomach growled and kept on growling. The ache grew worse. His bite wounds oddly didn't hurt that much. He attributed it to some kind of ointment Mary had applied when she stitched and bandaged him.

Fargo reached the door. He put an ear to it but he didn't hear so much as a snore. The latch scraped slightly. He listened at the crack but again heard nothing. Puzzled, he opened the door farther. The room beyond was dark. Not a single candle glowed. He thought he made out the fireplace in the far wall but the fire was out.

Given the cold and the snow, Fargo thought that strange. He opened the door even more and took a step, seeking some sign of where Tull and the Harpers were sleeping. The next instant his leg struck something, throwing him off balance. He grabbed at the wall to keep from falling but it was too late. Down he crashed, onto his hands and knees, and the knife went skittering.

A harsh laugh came out of the dark. A match flared and was held to the wick of a large candle. A glow spread across the floor, revealing Fargo. Revealing, too, a rope that had been stretched across the bottom of the door about six inches from the floor.

"Pretty slick if I say so myself," Tull declared, and came out of the shadows, his pearl-handled Colt in his hand.

Fargo spied Mary and the children, tied wrist and ankle and gagged, over in a corner.

"I didn't want them taking an ax to me in the middle of

the night," Tull said. "Or warning you." He chortled at his cleverness.

"You expected me to try something?"

"Let's just say I wasn't convinced you couldn't get out of that bed if you put your mind to it. So I took precautions."

Without being obvious, Fargo was searching for the toothpick. He thought it had slid to his right. The gleam of metal under a chair told him where it was. So far, Tull hadn't seen it. "I came out for a drink of water."

"You could have just hollered."

"And wake everyone up? I figured I could do it myself."

"Ain't you considerate," Tull scoffed. He moved to the table, swung a chair around, and straddled it. "Am I supposed to believe that?"

"Why wouldn't you?"

"Because that corn-haired filly yonder put a full pitcher and a glass on the dresser in the bedroom. I saw her with my own eyes."

"I didn't. I was out."

Tull scratched his chin with his Colt. "Now that I think of it, you were. You just might be telling the truth, seeing as how you don't have a weapon." He indicated a bucket on the counter. "Help yourself."

Fargo had to try twice to stand. Once again he swayed.

"Look at you. A puff of wind and you're liable to keel over."

"Can I untie the Harpers?"

"I'll do it in the morning when I wake up. Get your water and get back to bed."

Fargo took a few halting steps and deliberately swayed even worse. "I need to sit down or someone will have to carry me."

"Don't look at me." Tull pointed his Colt at the very chair the Arkansas toothpick was under. "Sit there. But as soon as you've caught your breath, get your damn water and get back into the damn bed."

Fargo put on a show of gratefully slumping down. He bent over with his elbows on his legs and bowed his head. "I'm about done in."

"I couldn't care less."

Fargo contrived to peer under the chair. The toothpick was just out of reach. He shifted slightly and slowly eased his hand down along the chair leg. He didn't think Tull noticed. He was wrong.

"What are you doing?"

"Just scratching an itch." Fargo straightened. He closed his eyes but not all the way.

Tull was staring suspiciously at the floor under the chair. Suddenly rising, he leveled his Colt. "Get up and take three steps back."

"What?"

"You heard me. And do it pronto or lose a knee."

Reluctantly, his hands out from his sides, Fargo counted the steps off. He could see the toothpick but it might as well be on the moon for all the good it was doing him.

Tull could see it, too. "What *is* that?" he demanded as he warily came over. He kicked the chair aside, and squatted. "Well, lookee here." He held the toothpick high so the blade caught the candle glow.

Fargo sensed what was coming and braced himself. "So this is what I get for sparing you? A knife in the gizzard?"

Tull rose. "You miserable son of a bitch."

Mary tried to say something through her gag.

"Shut up, cow," Tull snapped. He tossed the toothpick onto the table and advanced on Fargo, a vicious sneer curling his cruel face. "I've changed my mind, mister. If Cud wants to know who you are and what you were doing here, he can ask you in hell."

Fargo tried to dodge the boot rising toward his gut but he was too slow. Pain brought him to his knees. He flung out his arms to ward off a second kick and never saw the sweep of the Colt but he felt the blow to his temple. The next he knew, he was on his side with the killer gloating over him.

"Any last words, mister? Any begging you care to do? It won't change anything but you can grovel if you want."

Fargo glared.

"Tough bastard, is that it? Well, we'll see. It's been a while since I stomped anyone to death."

Over in the corner Mary and Nelly were trying to speak and thrashing wildly about.

"You're going to be a long time dying."

Jayce began kicking the wall.

"Cut that out!" Tull growled, not taking his eyes off Fargo. "All that fuss to keep me from kicking your teeth in. They must like you, mister. When I'm done, I'll give each of them a tooth as a keepsake."

Fargo placed his hands flat on the floor. He had one chance and one chance only.

"This is going to be fun," Tull said, and raised his boot.

7

Fargo stood no chance in a fight. He was too weak to last long. Tull knew it but he had overlooked one thing. Fargo didn't *have* to last if he could bring Tull down quickly. So as Tull raised his leg to stomp him, Fargo resorted to the dirtiest trick there was; he drove his fist up and in, slamming his knuckles into Tull's groin.

The killer cursed and staggered back. Sputtering, he clutched himself. His face became red, almost purple. "You're dead, you bastard." He tried to raise his pearl-handled Colt.

Fargo heaved off the floor. The movement made him light-headed, but he lashed out, swatting Tull's wrist just as the Colt went off. The revolver thundered loud in the confines of the cabin. The slug missed him and struck a wall.

"Kill you!" Tull railed, and thumbed back the hammer to try again.

Fargo punched him, a short, brutal chop to the throat that sent Tull crashing onto his side.

Now the sounds that came from Tull's throat weren't words. They were gurgles and snarls. He'd dropped the Colt and now he grabbed for it, his fingers rigid claws.

Bending, Fargo punched him again, in the side of the neck. Not once, but three times, and after the third blow Tull broke out in convulsions and loud whines burst from his gaping mouth.

Fargo reached for the Colt. He moved as slow as a turtle but he got it in his hand. He cocked it and placed the muzzle against Tull's forehead. "You shouldn't treat a lady like that." He squeezed the trigger.

The commotion in the corner had ceased. Mary and her young ones were gaping at the brains and hair and gore. Nelly made gagging sounds. Jayce laughed with glee.

Wincing, Fargo reclaimed his toothpick and shuffled over. "I'll have you free in a moment." Since he couldn't trust his legs, he sat down. Mary was on her knees, staring at him, and there was a question in her eyes. He removed the gag and threw the cloth aside. "Did he hurt you any?"

"No. I'm more worried about you. You're as white as a sheet."

Fargo nodded at the brains and the blood. "Sorry about the mess."

"He didn't give you a choice."

"You're safe now," Fargo said, and began carefully cutting the rope around her wrists.

"I wish that were true. But Cud Sten will be here soon. Tull was a friend of his. He won't like this one bit. And he won't care that you were defending yourself."

"Who says he has to find out?"

"You mean bury the body where Cud will never find it? That still leaves Tull's horse. I'd take it up into the mountains and leave it in a box canyon I know of—only with all the snow, it would starve."

"We can say the horse showed up by itself," Fargo suggested. "Then we'll show him the dead wolves and let him add two and two himself."

Mary smiled. "It just might work. So long as Cud doesn't catch on that you were the one the wolves nearly tore apart."

"So long as I don't go around naked, he won't suspect."

Her cheeks flushed pink and she gave a light cough. "You can wear some of Frank's clothes. You're taller than he was, so they might not fit all that well, but it's the best we can do."

The rope finally parted and Fargo gave the toothpick to her. He was on the brink of collapse. With difficulty, he stood and moved to the stove. The pot of chicken soup was cold but he didn't care. He took a ladle from a hook and carried the pot and the ladle and the Colt to the table. Setting the Colt down, he ate as one starved.

"You'd better chew that or you'll make yourself sick," Mary cautioned, coming over. She had cut Nelly free and Nelly was doing the same for her brother. "I can heat it if you'd like."

"No," Fargo said with his mouth crammed.

"Would you care for some coffee? I don't have much left but I'll put a pot on to brew."

Fargo was tempted but the coffee might keep him up and he needed sleep as much as he needed anything. "Maybe in the morning."

The children crossed to their mother and she draped her arms over their shoulders.

"I'm sorry you had to see that," Fargo told them. He meant it. Kids and horses—he didn't like to see either suffer.

Nelly shrugged. "It was no worse than that day we watched the grizzly eat our pa."

"I'd like to see you shoot him again," Jayce said. "He was mean to my ma. He had it coming."

Mary knelt and took hold of her son's hands. "Now who is being mean? No one ever deserves to die."

Fargo disagreed, and ladled more soup into his mouth to keep from saying so.

"But you're right in one respect," Mary went on. "Sometimes the only way to deal with men like Mr. Tull is to do what no one should ever have to do."

Fargo had lost count of the number of times he'd had to do it. The frontier was chock-full of Tulls. They came in all sizes and guises, and they all had one trait in common: They were heartless bastards who didn't care who they hurt.

"Now why don't the two of you scoot to bed while I take care of Mr. Tull?" Mary hugged and kissed first Nelly and then Jayce, and they headed for a door on the other side of the room.

"I'll help you," Fargo offered.

"You'll do no such thing. It would only make you worse." Mary stared down at the body. "It shouldn't be all that hard for me to drag him outside. In the morning I'll bury him if I can find a spot of ground soft enough."

Fargo hadn't thought of that. What with the cold and the snow, the ground would be rock hard. "That was a nice talk you gave your boy."

"You think so? He's young yet. He doesn't need to know the truth."

Puzzled, Fargo asked, "Which truth are we talking about?"

"Tull *did* deserve that bullet. He was as vicious as those wolves. The wolves, though, had an excuse. They were hungry. Tull was just a miserable son of a bitch who would have done the world a favor if he'd been stillborn."

The shock of her language took a few seconds to wear off so that Fargo could say, "And here I reckoned you were one of those weak sisters who sticks her head in the sand rather than take life as it is."

"I suppose I gave that impression. But it was for my son's and daughter's benefit. The harsh realities of life will beat on them soon enough. I don't see a reason to hurry it along."

Fargo found himself admiring her more and more. "One face for your kids and one for the mirror?"

"Something like that, yes," Mary answered with a grin. "You catch on quick. Are you a parent, yourself?"

"Hell, no. I'm not ready to set down roots." Then there was the little matter of meeting the right woman.

"It's hard, Skye. Harder than anything I've ever had to do, and that includes giving birth. But I wouldn't trade being a mother for all the ill-gotten gains Cud Sten makes from his rustling and robbing."

Fargo put a hand on the Colt. "I hope Tull has plenty of ammunition in his saddlebags."

Those lovely emerald eyes of her narrowed. "Surely you don't have the notion I think you're toying with? You're one man and he'll have seven or eight others with him. All as vicious as Tull."

"He's made your life miserable long enough."

"No, no, no," Mary said, shaking her head. "Besides the odds, there's the shape you're in."

"I can mend a lot before he gets here."

"But why? We hardly know each other."

"I like what I know. I like it a lot."

"Oh." Mary looked away. When she faced him again, there was the same question in her eyes. But she quickly recovered her composure. "You finish eating your food and I'll tuck you in."

"Yes, Ma," Fargo teased.

Mary laughed, the first real laugh he heard from her. She covered her mouth as if self-conscious of what she had done, then said, "You perplex me, sir. More than any man I ever met."

"Does that include your Frank?"

"Frank was a good man. He was devoted and hardworking. A simple man, some would say." Mary paused. "But I suspect there's nothing simple about you. There's nothing simple at all."

"I'm as ordinary as water."

Mary glanced at Tull. "Say what you will, but I know better." She went into the bedroom and came out with a blanket. Spreading it on the floor, she rolled Tull onto it. It took some doing. She was huffing when she was done. She placed Tull's hat on his chest and went to wrap the blanket around him.

"Wait." Fargo had eaten enough that newfound vitality was coursing through his veins. He got up and went over and hunkered. "Waste not, want not, I've heard folks say." He began to go through the dead man's pockets.

"I should have thought of it," Mary said.

Fargo found the usual. A pocketknife. A plug of tobacco. A crumpled letter he had no interest in. And a poke that jangled. He undid the tie string and upended the poke over the floor and out spilled double eagles and other coins and a wad of bills.

"My word, where did all that come from?"

"That rustling and robbing you were talking about, remember?" Fargo counted it. "Two hundred and forty-seven dollars."

"That's more than my Frank and I had at any one time in all the years we were married."

Fargo kept the forty-seven for himself. He put the two hundred back in the poke and placed it in her hand. "Here."

"What do you want me to do with it?"

"Whatever you want. It's yours."

Mary stared at it and trembled slightly. "I couldn't. It's not right."

"He sure as hell has no use for it."

"But like you say, he got it by dishonest means."

"So? If you knew where he got it from, you could give some of it back if it bothered you that much, but you don't. And it would be stupid to let it go to waste. It's yours, and that's that."

"Oh, Skye."

A tingle ran down Fargo's spine, startling him. "Don't make more of it than there is," he said more gruffly than he intended.

"Do you realize what this means for me and my children?"

Fargo patted the forty-seven dollars. "For me this means a

poker game and a bottle of whiskey." He unbuckled Tull's gun belt and stripped it off. Then he wrapped the body in the blanket, stood, and took hold of the shoulders. "You get the other end and we'll drag him out."

"You're in no condition," Mary warned. "I can do it myself."

"We don't have all night. My cold soup is getting colder, and I'd like to eat a little more before I turn in."

Reluctantly, Mary did as he wanted. Working together they hauled the body to the front door. Fargo was caked with sweat and could barely stand, but he opened the door and helped her push the body out. When he straightened, he swayed and had to the grip the wall to stay on his feet.

"See? I told you." Mary stood at his side and hooked her arm around his waist. "Lean on me. I'll get you to bed."

"You'll get me to the table. I told you I'm not done eating."

"Why are men so stubborn?"

"Why do women ask such silly questions?"

Mary grinned. She pushed the door shut with her foot and helped him to the chair, then sat in the one next to him. Her chin in her hands, she regarded him thoughtfully.

"Where will you go from here?" Fargo asked between mouthfuls. "With that money you can start a whole new life."

"Go? We don't have a horse, remember? Let alone three."

"Cud Sten does. I'm sure he and his men have lots of horses. Enough for all of you and for pack animals to take out your pots and pans and whatnot."

"I couldn't ask you to do that. Not if you're only doing it for me. I don't want you hurt on my account."

Fargo grinned a lopsided grin. "You can't take all the credit. There're the kids."

Mary looked into his eyes. "What kind of man are you?"

"The kind who needs a lot of sleep." Fargo's belly was about fit to explode and his eyelids had grown heavy.

"No. Really. I'd like to know."

"Hell." Fargo sat back. "I put my pants on one leg at a time, just like every other man."

Mary coughed, then said softly, "Thank you."

"Thank me in three or four days. This Cud Sten could turn out to be as tough as you say."

"He is. And he's got a man with him who is downright scary. Rika, they call him." Mary paused. "I was thinking we would hide you."

"Like you did with Tull?"

"Off in the trees. We could make you a lean-to."

"No."

"You can die, you know. Everyone will."

"We start dying the moment we're born. A couple days from now or a couple years, it all ends the same." The important thing to Fargo was that she and her kids weren't caught in a hail of lead.

"You worry me. You worry me considerably."

"Good," Fargo said, and grinned.

8

Fargo slept eighteen hours, and when he woke up, he was famished. He no sooner sat up than Mary entered the bedroom, smiling, and informed him she had a surprise. He thought it was the pile of clothes she had placed by the bed for him to pick from.

His buckskins had been ripped and torn in so many places that until he got the spare set out of his saddlebags or made new ones, he had to make do with a shirt and pants that belonged to her husband. Neither fit well. The pants, in particular, were too short, and too tight at the crotch. His manhood stood out as if sculpted, which made him grin.

His boots were okay to wear, and his gun belt was fine. The pearl-handled Colt fit nicely. Since it was the same caliber as his, he had plenty of ammunition. The Arkansas toothpick as always, went in his ankle sheath.

He had lost his hat somewhere so he put on a floppy one Frank Harper had used. It made him look so ridiculous that he decided to go without a hat.

Fargo stared at his image in the mirror and shook his head in amusement. He looked like he should be huddled in an alley, a wine bottle glued to his lips. His left arm and right leg were stiff from the bites, but the more he moved them, the better he felt. He practiced drawing the Colt a few times and slicked it as quick as could be.

Fargo went into the main room. There was the real surprise. Delicious aromas brought a roar from his stomach.

Two candles were on the table. Mary had set out her best plates, with a fork and a spoon beside each. A cup and saucer sat by the plate at the head of the table. She was cooking and humming, wearing what had to be the best dress she owned. Nelly and Jayce were over near the hearth, staring at her as if they couldn't quite believe what they were seeing.

"Are you hungry?" Mary asked.

"I could eat those wolves raw," Fargo said.

"No need for that." Mary brought the coffeepot over. "Permit me." She held out the chair for him, and after he sat, she filled the cup with steaming-hot coffee. "Courtesy of the late and never to be lamented Tull Fitch."

"Oh?"

"I went through his saddlebags and found coffee and flour and cornmeal and a few other things. Not a lot, but it will do us." Beaming, Mary beckoned. "Children, why don't you have a seat?"

They came over slowly, as if afraid the table would bite them, and sat staring at Fargo as if afraid he might bite them, too.

"Something the matter?" Fargo asked.

Nelly leaned closer and whispered, "What did you do to our ma?"

"I thanked her for the use of your pa's clothes."

Jayce fidgeted and regarded his mother with unease. "She's been acting different ever since she tucked you in."

"Different how?"

"Nice."

Fargo chuckled. "It could be she's just happy that Tull won't bother her anymore."

"She's happy about something but it's not that."

Mary placed a bowl of scrambled eggs on the table. She had also made flapjacks and johnnycakes. There was a plate of toast, smeared lightly in jam. For meat they had the left-over chicken. And for dessert, she informed them, there were iced pastries.

Jayce's eyes were wide with amazement. "We haven't ate this good since I can remember."

"When we get to a town and I find work, there will be more meals like this. Now dig in and help yourselves."

Fargo wolfed down the eggs. He didn't realize that he was the only one eating them until he was almost done. Then he noticed that they had all taken small portions of everything, leaving the lion's share for him. He put down his fork and sat back. "You have to be hungrier than that."

Mary was about to take a bite of toast. "Believe me, for us this is a feast."

"I'm no hog."

"You need to regain your strength." Mary smiled. "And it's my small way of saying thank you."

Fargo turned to the kids. "Help yourselves to more. If you don't, I won't take another bite."

"But Ma said—"

"Hush, son." Fargo reached across and put a slice of toast and a johnnycake on each of their plates.

"I have died and gone to heaven," Jayce said.

As the kids ate, now and then one or the other would close their eyes and make small sounds of pleasure. Mary, too, had a look of serene contentment.

Fargo could only begin to guess how rare this must have been. They were worse off than he thought. Toward the end of the meal, after Mary brought over the iced pastries, he asked something he had been wondering about. "Of all the places you could live, why did you and your husband pick here?"

"It was Frank's doing," Mary answered. "He wanted to get away from people. He wanted somewhere we could live in peace."

"The middle of the Beartooth Mountains?" Fargo never ceased to marvel at the ridiculous things people did.

A sheepish look came over her. "You have to understand. My Frank was very much his own man. He liked doing things his way. And he took great pride in being able to provide for us all by his lonesome."

Fargo gazed about the spare room and at their threadbare clothes. He almost asked, *You call this providing?* Only a harebrained idiot would think that bringing his family to the remote Bearthtooths was good for them. He suspected that Frank Harper had been one of those pigheaded sorts who had to do everything his way.

Mary had more to say. "Frank was a loner. I knew that when I married him, and I accepted it. No one is perfect. The few flaws he had were more than outweighed by his good qualities. A woman couldn't ask for a more kind and considerate father to her children. And he always did his best for us."

"I'm glad you were happy."

"I was, Skye. Really and truly. Oh, we didn't have much, but we had one another, and that counted more to me than anything."

Jayce said, "I loved my pa."

"Me, too," Nelly threw in.

Fargo let it drop. It wasn't any of his business, anyhow. He finished eating, pushed back his plate, and patted his belly. "That was about one of the best meals I ever ate."

Mary was pleased. "I have another surprise for you, but it doesn't have to do with food." She went to a closet and came back holding something behind her. "You mentioned that you lost your rifle when you lost your horse. Maybe this will do until you can find them." She held out a Sharps rifle. "This was in Tull's saddle scabbard."

Fargo grinned in delight. He'd used a Sharps for a spell once, and liked it a lot. They held only one shot, but the

heavier-caliber models were powerful enough to drop a buffalo or a grizzly.

"And you'll need these."

In a leather bag was enough ammunition to hold off a
war party. Fargo loaded the Sharps and leaned it against his
chair. "I'll go hunting in the morning." They had done so
much for him, the least he could do was put meat on their
table.

Mary sat back down. "I've been thinking," she said hesi-
tantly. "Tull's horse is tied out back."

"So?"

"You could be long gone when Cud Sten and his men get
here."

Fargo looked at her. She was asking him to run out on
them. "That's a hell of a thing to say to me."

Mary averted her gaze. "It's just that they're likely to kill
you if you stay. Cud has had his sights set on me for some
time. He'll be jealous, you staying under our roof. Then
there's Tull. No one ever kills one of Cud Sten's men and
lives. He brags about that."

The way Fargo saw it, he could do one of three things. He
could hide nearby and wait for Sten's bunch to leave. He could
stay put and give a good account of himself. Or he could
play cat and mouse. "Has he ever laid a hand on you?"

Mary flushed. "Not yet, but not through lack of interest.
The reason he keeps coming back is that he wants me to be
his woman. He told me so to my face. He even hinted that if
I don't give in, he might take me by force."

"I figured as much."

"I told him that if he ever tried, I would get hold of a knife
and cut off parts of him he's partial to. So far, the threat has
kept his hands off me."

Fargo was blunt with her. "It won't do so forever."

"No," Mary agreed. "Why is why I've been praying for a
miracle." She added in a low voice, "And here you are."

Fargo figured she was joking until he saw the look on her face. "I doubt the Almighty brought me here."

"I take it you're not a religious man? Well, I can't claim to be all that God-fearing myself. But I *have* been praying for deliverance, and there you sit, willing to help us. If that's not a miracle, I don't know what is."

Fargo wasn't one of those people who saw omens in everyday occurrences. Some Indian tribes did. An owl would fly over their village, and they would take that as a sign of good fortune. To him, it was just an owl that happened to fly past at that moment. Some whites were the same way. A man dying of thirst in the desert might stumble on a tank in the rocks and call it divine deliverance. To Fargo, it was coincidence or a lot of luck.

"Be that as it may," Mary was saying, "I don't want you hurt on my account. Sorry, on *our* account."

Nelly broke in with, "I don't want you hurt, either."

"Me, either," Jayce evidently felt obliged to add.

Fargo swallowed some coffee and put his cup on the saucer. "There's just one thing I need to know. Do you want to get out of here or not?"

Mary sighed. "Have we had enough of mountain life? Of barely scraping by? Of going days without food? Of not having decent clothes? Of having to haul water from the stream? Are we tired of the scorching heat of summer and the freezing cold of winter? Of having to chop down a forest of wood to make it through until spring?" She paused. "What do you think?"

"I want out of here so much, I cry myself to sleep at night," Nelly said softly.

"I sort of like it," Jayce said. "except for the bears and the mountain lions and the wolves. Oh, and the rattlesnakes. Oh, and the hostiles, too."

Fargo nodded. "I'll get you out, but you have to abide by

what I say. We do things my way and only my way." Otherwise they were likely to get themselves killed.

Mary looked at her children. "He's saying it will be dangerous. He's saying we could die."

"Whatever you need, Mr. Fargo," Nelly said.

"I'll do whatever Ma says to do," was Jayce's response.

Fargo pushed back his chair. Thanks to the sleep and the food, he truly felt like a new man. His wounds hurt but he had always been good at bearing pain. "I'm going for a ride," he announced. "I want to look the valley over."

Mary quickly said, "I can go with you to show you around if you'd like. That is, if you don't mind riding double."

"I reckon I could put up with you," Fargo said with a grin. "But the kids aren't to step out that door until we get back."

"You heard him," Mary said.

"Yes, Ma."

"What if I have to. . . . you know?"

"Then you use the outhouse. But you scoot right back inside and you keep the door barred."

Tull's horse was a sorrel. It was in a corral made of trimmed limbs at the back of the cabin. The saddle and saddle blanket had been hung over the top rail. Fargo went up to the horse and patted it, taking its measure. Some horses spooked easy or were biters or would as soon stomp a man to death as let him ride them. The sorrel seemed to have a good disposition. It didn't fight the bridle, and it stood still as he threw the saddle blanket on.

"Let me," Mary said, coming up beside him. She had a red shawl over her shoulders and an old blue bonnet on her head. What with her golden hair and her green eyes, she compared favorably to other beauties Fargo had known.

"I'm not helpless."

"Oh, I forgot. You're male."

Grinning, Fargo swung the saddle on top of the saddle blanket. He raised the stirrup and did the cinch.

"We can take as long as you want looking around," Mary said. "I told Nelly and Jayce we might be awhile."

"Did you?" Fargo asked, and was rewarded with another blush.

"I didn't know what you have in mind. I mean, how far you want to go. Or how much you want to see."

"I want to go all the way." Fargo locked eyes with her. "I want to see all there is to see."

"I'm at your disposal." Mary's blush deepened.

Before climbing on, Fargo shoved the Sharps into the scabbard. He gritted his teeth, gripped the saddle horn, and forked leather, expecting the pain to be a lot worse than it turned out to be. Leaning down, he offered his hand.

"Are you sure? I can do it myself. I don't want to hurt you."

Fargo hoisted her up. A tap of his spurs and they were out of the corral. She looped her arms around his waist.

"I haven't had time to myself in a coon's age," Mary mentioned. "This will be a treat. If only it wasn't so bitterly cold."

"Don't worry," Fargo said. "I have ways of keeping us warm."

9

Frank Harper had built the cabin fifty yards from the nearest stream. He could have built it closer for convenience, but as Mary explained to Fargo, "My husband thought it best if the cabin was deep in the trees. He figured we were less likely to be visited by hostiles."

Fargo grunted. Yes, the cabin was well hidden, but the smoke from the chimney gave their presence away just as surely.

The valley floor was mostly open. Again, Frank had liked it that way. "He had dreams of a big cattle ranch someday," Mary related. "With hundreds of heads of cattle."

Again Fargo grunted. Even if Frank Harper's dream had come true, it would have taken Harper weeks—no, months— to get his cattle to market, and by the time he got them there, the cows would be so worn-out, it was doubtful he would get top dollar.

The more Fargo learned of Frank Harper, the more the man impressed him as one of those dreamers whose grand schemes seldom amounted to much.

"Frank figured that one day there'll be towns and settlements out here. We'd be well set by then, and live prosperous and happy."

Again Fargo grunted.

"Why do you keep doing that? Didn't my food agree with you?"

"I've never tasted better."

"It's my husband, isn't it? You don't agree with how he thought things would be."

Fargo shrugged and felt his shoulder blades rub her bosom. "There's an old saying about not speaking ill of the dead."

"I'm a grown woman. I can take it."

Fargo turned his head to look at her. Her face was so close, his mouth almost brushed her cheek. "Your husband was a good man. He tried to do right by you and the kids." He chose his next comment carefully. "But he wasn't very practical."

"No, he wasn't. He had his head in the clouds. I didn't want to come here. I honestly didn't. But he had his heart set on it. He believed we'd be happy and I let him convince me we would, even though I knew how hard we would have it."

"A lot of men would give anything to have a wife like you."

"What a nice thing to say." Mary paused. "How about you? Any plans to ever get hitched?"

Fargo suppressed the urge to grin. "No."

"Not ever in your entire life long?"

"None whatsoever."

"Oh."

They rode in silence for a bit save for the clomp of the sorrel's hooves and the swish of the snow. Ahead, a flurry of black wings rose from the first of the dead wolves.

"How do they do that?" Mary wondered. "How do they find dead things to eat in all this vast emptiness?"

Fargo shrugged again. He liked rubbing against her. "Buzzards have their ways."

A half dozen were feasting on the second wolf. They rose into the air as Fargo rode up.

"Look at that. They've picked it down to the bone. Another week and you'd never know there had been a live animal."

Fargo couldn't seem to stop grunting. He rode on, to near the bottom of the cliff, and gazed up in wonder, amazed he had survived the fall.

"You slid over *that*?" Mary asked.

Fargo pointed at the hole in the snow where he had hit. The proximity of several boulders made him queasy.

"You were awful lucky. Either that, or the Good Lord was watching over you."

"Don't start with that miracle stuff."

"As you wish. But you've got to admit you're lucky to be breathing."

"We all are," Fargo said. He reined along the base of the mountain and presently came on horse tracks that came down the slope and pointed in the direction of the Harper place.

"Tull's," Mary guessed.

There were no others. Nor did Fargo find any in the circuit he made of the valley. Eventually they came back to the stream, and Fargo stopped to let the sorrel drink. They both climbed down. He stepped to the water and saw that it was frozen along the edges. All it would take was for the temperature to fall a few more degrees and the entire stream would freeze.

Mary had her arms around herself and was stamping her feet. He could see her breath.

"Mercy me, it's cold. I can't wait to sit next to the fire."

The cold didn't bother Fargo as much. He was used to it. But it gave him second thoughts about a notion he was entertaining. He sighed in disappointment, and they climbed back on and rode to the corral. She waited while he stripped the sorrel, and she opened the door for him since his hands were full with the saddle and saddle blanket.

Nelly and Jayce bounded over to meet them and pestered their mother with questions about what they had seen on their ride. When Jayce heard about the buzzards, he wanted to go shoot them, but Mary told him that buzzards had to eat, too, and to leave them be. She put the coffeepot on to reheat and told Fargo to sit in a chair in front of the hearth.

Fargo extended his legs and felt the warmth creep up his boots to his ankles. He had a few decision to make, and he was deep in thought when Mary brought a steaming cup over. "We need to talk. Pull up a chair."

"No need." Mary sank down with her elbows on her knees and gazed up at him. The firelight lent her face a soft beauty fit to be captured on canvas. "I'm all ears."

Fargo took a slow sip. She was more than ears. She was as fine a woman as he ever met, and he found himself growing more fond of her than he should. He admired the luster of her hair and the fullness of her lips, and shook himself.

"Is something the matter?" Mary asked. "Didn't I make the coffee strong enough?"

"It's fine." Then, to take his mind off her and her hair, Fargo said, "We need to be clear on a few things. Do you and your kids realize what it will be like when we leave?"

Mary glanced at where Nelly and Jayce were playing dominoes at the table. "We want it more than anything."

"That's not what I asked."

"Sorry. What?"

"It's the dead of winter, Mary. Game will be hard to come by. We could starve before we make it out of the Beartooths. Or freeze to death. It won't be easy."

"We're aware of that. But we're willing to take the chance if you're willing to help us."

"Then there are the horses. Cud Sten won't hand them over to us. We'll have to take them. And he won't let us do that while he's still breathing. You know what that means. And your kids will be caught in the middle. Do you want that?"

"Can I live with the killing? Do I accept all the risks? Is that what you're asking me?"

Fargo almost grunted. Instead, he nodded.

Mary gazed into the fire. "There was a time when I'd have been horrified. I never liked the idea of killing. The meat on my plate when I was growing up? I refused to think of how it got there." She smiled a wistful smile. "But living out here has taught me how silly I was. The real world isn't as nice as we like to pretend it is. Everything kills in order to survive. Killing is as much a part of life as, well, life itself. So the idea no longer shocks me."

"Then you can do what you'll have to?"

"So long as you promise to keep Nelly and Jayce out of it as much as possible. I don't want them in any danger if it can be helped."

Fargo drummed his fingers on the chair. That changed things. He'd figured to let the Sten gang ride in and, when they were nice and comfortable, catch them off guard. But now she only left him one choice. "I'll ride out to meet them before they get here."

"Just you against Cud and all his men?"

"It's the only way to keep the kids out of it."

"I'm sorry. I'm making things harder for you, aren't I? We can do it some other way."

"That's the thing," Fargo said. There *was* no other way that would ensure that the kids were out of danger. Even at that, he couldn't guarantee it would turn out as he planned. He mentioned as much.

"I understand, and I thank you for being so honest with me. You have some fine qualities about you, Mr. Fargo. Offering to help us and not expecting anything in return."

"I never said that." Fargo roamed his eyes over her body in a manner that left no doubt what he was thinking.

"Oh, my." Mary coughed. "You come right out with it, don't you?"

"A man never gets a woman to part her legs by being shy."

"Is that all it would be to you? A bout of animal lust? Another poke to add to your tally?"

"For me it would be all there is that counts in this life." Fargo grinned. "Fine whiskey comes close."

Despite herself, Mary returned the grin. "You are a silver-tongued devil, I'll give you that. But I need you to understand. It won't be easy for me. I've never done anything like this in all my life."

"I'm not forcing you." Fargo wanted that clear.

"Oh, I know. I'm a fish, and you're holding out a worm and leaving it to me to decide whether I take the bait or not."

"No. You're a woman who hasn't been with a man in a year, and I'm a man who likes women."

"That's all there is? Our feelings don't enter into it?"

"That's up to you."

Mary didn't seem to hear him. "I mean, yes, I'm a woman. And to a woman, feelings are important. We don't just *do* it. Well, maybe some women do, for money, mostly, but I've never done that, and I never will. I'm not that kind of woman. I don't have it in me."

"All you have to say is no."

His voice seemed to startle her. She glanced up and then quickly looked away. "I didn't say that. I'm only making clear how hard something like this is for someone who only ever gave herself to one man her whole life. Can you appreciate that? What it's like for me?"

Fargo nodded. "You're trying to decide whether you want to let down your hair for an hour or keep bottling it up."

Mary was spared having to reply by Jayce, who came skipping over to announce that he had beaten his sister at dominoes.

"That's nice, son, but you shouldn't gloat. Be as courteous when you win as you are when you lose."

"When I lose I'm grumpy."

Mary tousled his hair and pecked him on the cheek. "I'll

tell you what. Why don't you keep our guest company while I fix supper? And tonight when I tuck you in, I have a special surprise."

"What kind of surprise?"

Mary stood and patted his head and moved toward the counter.

"Ever notice, Mr. Fargo, how girls talk your ears off except when you want them to say something?"

"Learned that already, have you?" Fargo chuckled. "It's one of the three great lessons of life."

"What are the other two?"

"Always fold when the other player asks for one card and then wets himself raising."

"I don't get that. What's the other lesson?"

"Never try to talk a dove out of her price. She'll take it as an insult and only pretend she likes it."

Jayce scratched his head. "Gosh. I don't get that one, either. Where did you learn these lessons?"

"I learned the one about folding in St. Louis. I stayed in and lost nearly every cent I had to a full house."

"I don't know what that is. And the bird?"

"The bird?" Fargo repeated, and snorted. "No, not that kind of dove. The doves I'm talking about don't have feathers."

"Naked birds? They have such a thing?"

"Did your pa ever have a special talk with you?"

"We had a lot of talks. About farming and hunting and fishing and the stars and how frogs are tadpoles before they're frogs and why some caterpillars change into butterflies and how come people snore."

"The talk I'm thinking of was about where babies come from. Or maybe it was calves and foals."

Jayce brightened. "We had that talk, too. Pa sat me down one day and got all serious and said he was going to tell me how Nelly and me came into the world."

"What did he say?"

"The stork brought us."

"Go away."

"What?"

"Go play with your sister."

"Why? What did I do? Don't you like storks?"

"I want to take a nap before we eat." Fargo was feeling tired from the long ride. He wasn't quite himself yet.

"Oh. Sure." Jayce took a step, then stopped. "I miss my pa. I miss our talks. You remind me of him a little. And I thank you for the lessons, even if they didn't make any kind of sense."

"Your mother wouldn't happen to have a whiskey bottle hidden around here somewhere, would she?"

"Not that I know of. Why do you ask?"

10

The children were asleep and their door was closed. Flames crackled in the stone hearth. Outside, the night wind shrieked down off the mountains and on across the valley. Wolves tried to compete and couldn't.

Fargo sat in a chair facing the fireplace. His eyes were closed, his chin bobbed. He was tired and ready for bed. It had been a long day. He'd held up well, but it would be a few days yet before he recovered enough from his wounds to be his old self. A noise made him turn his head. It came from the bedroom he was using: Mary's bedroom. She had excused herself a while ago and gone in. She didn't say why. He figured she was getting ready for bed.

Supper had consisted of another chicken and fresh bread. Fargo had taken small portions and didn't ask for seconds so there was enough for all of them. The kids had been too busy stuffing their faces to notice. If Mary did, she didn't say anything.

Fargo stared into the dancing flames. He needed a good night's sleep so he could get an early start. He had a plan—a crazy plan as Mary called it—but if it worked, she and the kids would be free to go wherever their hearts desired, and be free of the claws of Cud Sten, as well.

Another noise from the bedroom caused Fargo to turn, and for a few seconds he was breathless with desire. Then he caught himself and quietly asked, "You did all that for me?"

Mary Harper had changed into a nightgown. Where many

gowns were loose-fitting and bulky, this was tight and scandalously sheer. It was bright red, matching the red of her cheeks. She had brushed her hair and done things with her face so that she appeared as fresh as a new-bloomed daisy. Nervously clasping her hands in front of her, she said demurely, "Frank got this for me so I could treat him now and then, as he put it."

Fargo's estimation of the man rose considerably.

"I know I don't look like much but it's the very best thing I own."

"Come here," Fargo huskily requested.

With a glance at the door to the kids' bedroom, she crossed and stood timidly beside the chair, her eyes downcast.

"What's wrong?"

"I told you. The only other man I've ever been with was Frank. I'm scared out of my wits. You'd think I wouldn't be, given I've had two kids and all. But this is nothing like being married. This is"—Mary paused as if seeking the right word—"exciting."

Fargo put his hand on her wrist.

"Wait. There are rules."

"Rules?"

"I don't want Nelly and Jayce to hear us. We have to be quiet. And we go in my bedroom and throw the bolt so one of them doesn't walk in on us. And if they knock, we stop right away and I get dressed and get out of bed to see what they want."

"Anything else?"

Her eyes were pools of uncertainty. "You won't hurt me, will you? I mean, you're not one of those? My Frank was always gentle. That's how I like it. Nice and easy and gentle."

"I'm not Frank," Fargo said, and pulled her into his lap. She resisted for the briefest instant. Then her bottom was on his manhood and his mouth was molded to hers. She gasped and in doing so parted her lips, enabling him to slide his tongue into her mouth.

Mary was momentarily taken aback. She pressed against his shoulders, but not hard, and cooed deep in her throat. Slowly, she melted against him, until her mouth was molten with need.

They kissed and they kissed. It was Fargo who broke for air. Mary rested her cheek on his chest and shook from head to toe.

"Oh, my."

"What?"

"Frank never kissed like that."

"I'm not Frank," Fargo repeated. He caressed her hair and ran his other hand down to the small of her back. She sat still, her hands in her lap, a frightened bird ready to take wing. "You can relax."

"That's easy for you to say. If my children caught us, I'd be embarrassed beyond tears. They mean everything to me, Skye. And I do mean everything."

Mary gazed about the room. "We may not have much but we've always had love and respect. I wouldn't want to lose that."

Fargo could take a hint. Scooping her into his arms, he rose and moved toward her bedroom.

"There's no need to carry me. I can walk."

"I've known chipmunks that chattered less," Fargo said by way of making her hush.

"I can't help it. It's all I can do to keep from trembling like a newlywed." Mary touched a fingertip to his lips. "Be patient with me, please. I'll try not to disappoint you."

Fargo set her on her feet and she timidly craned her neck to kiss him. He slid his hands behind her, gripped her bottom, and ground against her.

"Goodness! Be gentle, remember?"

Fargo squeezed her harder, then hauled off and gave her

bottom a slap. She arched her back and her eyes widened in surprise . . . and something else.

"You call that gentle?"

Roving a hand to her belly, Fargo rubbed in circles until his hand brushed a breast. He covered it with his palm. Her nipple was growing as hard as a tack. When he pinched it, her eyelids fluttered and she mewed in delight. "Liked that, did you?"

"You make me tingle."

Fargo intended to do a lot more than that. He eased her onto the bed on her back and was about to spread out next to her.

"The bolt, remember?"

Grumbling, Fargo hurried to the door and back again. He removed his spurs. He'd torn apart more than a few quilts, blankets, and sheets in his time, and she didn't have any to spare.

"Lord, I hope I'm not making the biggest mistake of my life. If words get around, I'll have men crawling out of the woodwork, thinking I'm easy."

"Who is there to tell?" Fargo unbuckled his gun belt and set it to one side. He was rock-hard under his pants, so hard it hurt, a delicious hurt he could never get enough of. He commenced kissing her; her throat, her cheeks, her brow. Her body grew hot. She squirmed in rising delight and sank her fingernails into his shoulders.

Fargo's mouth found hers. He covered her mounds and kneaded them through the sheer fabric of her nightgown. She bit his bottom lip as if trying to devour him, then suddenly drew back, her eyes widening in horror.

"Oh, no."

Not having any idea what she was upset about, and not caring to stop, Fargo went to nuzzle her neck and was surprised when she pushed against his chest, stopping him. "What's the matter?"

"I bit you so hard, there's a drop of blood."

Fargo didn't understand why she was so disturbed. "Bite me all you want. Just so you don't rip my throat open."

"I didn't mean to do it."

Drawing back, Fargo stared. "A drop of blood never hurt anybody. What's really got you upset?"

"I—" Mary hesitated. "I lost control."

"All you did was bite me."

"I never bit Frank's lip."

"I keep telling you I'm not Frank. Bite me, claw me, pull my hair out—it won't make me faint."

"It's not you," Mary said. "It's me."

"I don't savvy."

"Aren't you listening? I lost *control*. I got so excited, I bit you without thinking. I've never, ever done that my whole life."

"Calm down. It's not as if you ripped my clothes off and had your way with me."

"That's just it. I want to."

To Fargo's delight, she threw an arm around his neck and pulled him to her. She kissed him fiercely, moaning all the while, and did the last thing he expected her to do: She reached between his legs and cupped his rigid pole. Her lips and her body were living fire. She didn't so much make love to him as consume him.

Time lost all meaning. Mary kissed and rubbed and stroked and aroused as few women had ever done to Fargo. He held his own for a while and then lay back and let her do as she pleased. She pleased to do everything. Her lips roved everywhere. She was a bottomless wellspring of carnal craving, and she craved to be filled.

When, at long last, they neared the peak, Fargo throbbed with the need for release. His manhood felt fit to rupture.

Mary crested first. She threw back her head and her eyes widened in amazement, and then she bit her lip to keep from crying out as she bucked and heaved and cooed and gushed, gushed, gushed.

Her climax triggered Fargo's. He hurtled over the brink, surprised by the intensity. It was like no time, ever. It was different. It was unique. It was the best.

They coasted to a stop and Fargo collapsed beside her. That was the last he knew until a gentle shaking of his arm brought him out of perhaps the deepest sleep of his life to find her gazing lovingly into his eyes.

"Good morning."

"What?" Fargo thought she was mistaken. They couldn't have slept that long.

"It's almost dawn. Half an hour and the sun will rise. I've checked on Nelly and Jayce, and they're still sound asleep."

Groggily, Fargo raised up and looked around. "I slept the whole night?" He sank back down.

"What was left of it. We were up pretty late." Mary tenderly touched his cheek. "Thank you."

"Anytime."

"That was like nothing I've ever experienced. I thought that Frank and I—" Mary stopped. "How do I put this?"

"It's never the same with any two people."

"No. I don't mean that." Mary's brow puckered. "I thought I knew what it was all about. I mean, Frank and I did it, well, fairly often." She touched him again, a great tenderness on her face. "But none of those times were anything like this. I don't know if I can describe it in words."

"There's no need." Fargo closed his eyes. If they had half an hour until daylight, he might as well get a little more sleep.

Mary kissed his cheek, his chin, his throat. "If I could, I would do it again right this minute. But the children will be up soon."

"Rest," Fargo said.

"I don't want rest. I want you. I want you again and again. I want you until I pass out."

Fargo looked at her, and damn if she wasn't serious. "I won't complain if you take it into your head to ravish me again sometime."

"How about tonight?"

"If I make it back."

Mary pressed her mouth to his, hard. "How about every night for the rest of our lives?"

Fargo sobered and propped his head on his arm. "I thought I made it clear. I'm not looking to put down roots."

"I'd make you happy. I'd make you as happy as any man has ever been since the dawn of time."

"Oh, Mary . . ."

"Think about it. That's all I ask. Think about it, and if you want, stick around awhile and make up your mind."

"I'm taking you and your kids out of here, remember?"

"There's no rush. With you here we'll have plenty to eat. You'll hunt game, and I'll cook and clean, and at night we'll do what we did last night, over and over. There will be no end to it. No end to us."

Fargo rolled onto his back and covered his eyes with his forearm. He liked her. He liked her a lot. Maybe it was even more than liking. There was no denying their coupling had been special. But what she was asking was impossible. He would eventually move on, as he always did.

"I've upset you, haven't I?"

"No," Fargo lied.

"Yes, I have. I can tell. I'm sorry. Truly sorry. It's the last thing I want to do." Mary rested her cheek on his neck.

Fargo was startled to feel a spot of wet on his skin. He peered from under his arm and saw tears trickling from the corners of her eyes. "Stop that."

"I don't want to lose you. This is so new, so wonderful. I've never known anything like it"

"I'm not the only man in the world," Fargo said by way of suggesting she would find someone else one day.

"You are for me. Don't you understand? What we have comes along only once or twice in a lifetime. It's rare. If we go our separate ways, we might never have it again."

Fargo draped his arm around her shoulders. "It's new for you. You're making more out of it than there is."

"You don't see. You just don't see."

"Mary, please."

Mary tilted her head to look at him. The tears were still flowing but she didn't sob or blubber. They were quiet tears. "I'll make this as clear to you as I possibly can. Then it's up to you to decide what you'll do about it." She cleared her throat.

"Don't."

"Skye Fargo, I love you."

"Oh, hell."

11

Fargo rode out half an hour after breakfast. He ate sparingly. They were running out of food. There wasn't much of the flour left, and Mary was reluctant to kill another chicken. He made up for the lack with half a pot of coffee.

The three of them came out to see him off. The cold had abated somewhat, thanks to warmer wind from the south.

Fargo was about to step into the stirrups when Mary came over and, in front of the children, kissed him warmly on the cheek.

"Take care and come back safe."

Fargo said he would try. He climbed on and looked down and felt a strange constriction in his throat. "If I don't make it back and Cud Sten shows up, wait for your chance and steal three horses and head out of the Beartooth Range." They wouldn't last another six months, otherwise.

Mary put her hand on his leg. "You'll come back. I know you will."

Fargo used his spurs. He looked back once and they were still standing at the corner of the cabin. All three waved. He waved back, then swore.

Fargo told himself he was upset because of Mary. She had forgotten that he told her that he had no interest in planting roots. He'd meant what he said but she refused to listen.

With a toss of his head, Fargo focused on the here and now. He made for a point where two mountains seemed to merge. Mary had told him that between them wound a strip of grassy flatland. It was the easiest way in and out of the valley, the way Cud Sten was likely to bring the cattle.

Once he reached the flatland, Fargo stayed close to the forest so he could seek cover quickly if he had to.

The snow had turned the mountains white. Here and there boulders added a splash of brown and pines a dash of green.

There was no sign of the outlaws.

The middle of the morning came and went. Fargo arched his back to relieve stiff muscles. He looked up at a pair of ravens flying overhead, their wings beating loud in the thin air. He looked down and drew rein.

Fresh tracks marked the snow, the prints of a single horse. A shod horse. It had come down off the mountain and set off across the flatland.

Fargo rose in the stirrups. The horse wasn't in sight. He reckoned it had gone into the forest on the other side. Sliding to the ground, Fargo hunkered down. A tingle shot through him and he was back on the sorrel in an instant. Then he hesitated. He wanted to go after the other horse. But Sten might come along while he was gone. Did he dare risk it? he asked himself. The answer was no. He had to put Mary and her kids first. It bothered him, though. He rode on with a heavy heart, glancing often across the flatland in the hope that the other horse would appear.

The sun was directly overhead when, faint on Fargo's ears, fell the lowing of a cow. Wasting no time, he reined into the snow-shrouded trees and behind a pine half bent from the weight. By craning his neck he could see over it.

Presently, here they came: seven riders herding a handful of cows.

Mary had told Fargo there would only be five or six men. Somewhere or other, Cud Sten had added new curly wolves to his pack.

Figuring out which rider was Sten was easy. He was the

only one holding—of all things—a club. About two feet long, it was thick at one end and tapered at the other. Oak, unless Fargo missed his guess. Why in the hell anyone would tote something like that around, Fargo couldn't imagine. A six-shooter killed a lot quicker. Sten also wore a revolver, butt-forward on his left hip. A Smith & Wesson.

Comparing the others to wolves wasn't far from the mark. All were lean and sinewy with eyes that glittered with the promise of death. Five were white. The sixth, who happened to be in the lead, had some red blood, as evinced by a shock of raven hair and copper skin.

The outlaws were herding the cows along but they weren't in any particular hurry. One man dozed in the saddle.

The half-breed was on a claybank. He came abreast of where Fargo was hidden and suddenly drew rein and leaned down.

Cud Sten stopped, too, rumbling "What is it, Rika? We've got us a ways to go yet and I want to be there by nightfall."

Rika straightened and turned. "Tracks," he said simply. "They puzzle me."

"How can that be?" Cud said. "What you don't know about tracking ain't worth knowing."

"A white man has come this way."

"What's that?" Cud said, and he and the rest glanced all about, most placing their hands on their revolvers.

"It's a white man we know," Rika said. "Or his horse, at least."

"What are you babbling about, damn it?"

Rika pointed at the tracks. "These were made by the animal our friend Tull rides."

"Are you sure?"

"As you say. What I don't know about tracking is not worth knowing. And I know the tracks of our horses as I know my own."

83

"But if it's Tull, where did he get to?"

"I ask myself the same question."

Cud gigged his bay up and the two of them climbed down and hunkered to examine the prints.

Fargo palmed the pearl-handled Colt. He knew what they would do next, and he was ready. They would mount and come after him. With luck he could drop half of them before they suspected where he was, and then it would be cat and mouse until he finished them off.

True to his prediction, Cud Sten and Rika whispered back and forth. They climbed on their horses and reined around to talk in hushed tones to the others. Then, drawing their six-shooters, all seven swung toward the forest.

They were so obvious Fargo had to grin. But he didn't find what happened next the least bit funny.

The branches of the pine were laden thick with snow. Now and then clumps fell to the ground. But just as the outlaws reined toward the forest, a clump of snow the size of a washbasin fell with a loud thud, and the pine, relieved of the weight, suddenly whipped straight up into the air. The rest of the snow in its branches came raining down on Fargo. For a few seconds all he saw was falling snow. Then the whiteout ended, and he could see again.

The tree no longer hid him.

He was in plain sight.

For a few seconds the outlaws were riveted in surprise. Then Cud Sten bellowed, "That's not Tull! Kill the son of a bitch!"

Fargo wheeled the sorrel and jabbed his spurs. Behind him six-guns blasted and lead sang a song of death. One buzzed his ear, another narrowly missed his shoulder. Then he was past more trees and at a gallop.

Cud Sten let out with another bellow. "After him!"

Fargo scowled. Thanks to a fluke he was riding for his

life. He reined right to avoid a tree, reined left to avoid another. A few more shots were fired but none came close. Then the shooting stopped.

The outlaws were after him in earnest.

The snow muffled the thud of their hooves. Nearly everything was white, the trees so burdened that many hung low to the ground. Fargo hadn't gone far when he discovered how precariously balanced they were. The sorrel brushed against one, and it snapped vertical as that first tree had done, raining snow all over him. .

"Don't let that son of a bitch get away!" Cud Sten bellowed.

Fargo glanced back. Two of them were hard after him. One raised a revolver but lowered it again because he didn't have a clear shot.

Minutes passed, and the sorrel's lead began to widen. But Fargo could tell the sorrel was beginning to tire. The heavy snow was sapping its vitality.

Fargo had to try something. He looked for another large pine, bent low, and soon spied a huge one so covered with snow, it resembled a white hill more than a tree. Reining around it, he came to a stop and hunched low over his saddle. Now it was up to fickle fate, which had already betrayed him once.

Off to the right hooves drummed. One of the outlaws flew past without seeing him.

To the left, more hooves. That made two.

Tense with hope, Fargo waited. Another rider was briefly visible, staring straight ahead. He heard one crash through the growth and twisted his head. The man had bushy red hair and a bushy red beard and, like the others, didn't notice him. That made four.

Only two to go and Fargo would be safe.

A man in a mackinaw went past.

Then it was Cud Sten himself, his club held high as if he couldn't wait to bash in Fargo's skull.

Fargo waited. He didn't hear the seventh. After a bit he decided the man must have gone by without him noticing and he gigged the horse around the pine.

Rika was barely ten feet away, the stock of a rifle wedged to his shoulder. The instant Fargo appeared, he fixed a bead on Fargo's head and said quietly, "It's up to you."

Fargo had the Colt at his side. He could jerk it up and fire, but he had no doubt that even if he got off a shot, he was as good as dead. Rika wouldn't miss, not at that range. "Don't do anything I'll regret," he said, smiling. Then, holding the Colt by two fingers, he slowly raised his hand and slid it into his holster. "There. How's that?"

Using only his legs, Rika goaded his horse nearer. "Turn so your back is to me and hold our arms out from your sides."

Fargo did so, chafing inside at his run of bad luck. He felt a slight tug on his holster. The pearl-handled Colt was gone.

"You can turn around now."

Rika had moved back out of reach and lowered the rifle to his waist, but it was still fixed on Fargo's chest. He hefted the Colt. "This belonged to a friend of mine. That horse is his, too. How is it you have them?"

"I lost my horse in the blizzard. I about died from the cold and the snow, and then I came on this animal and a man lying dead with a broken arrow stuck in him."

Rika's face showed no hint of whether he bought the story. "And why is it you were hiding behind that tree when we came by?"

Fargo shrugged. "I was on my way out of the mountains. I heard you and your friends coming and didn't know if you'd be friendly."

Again Rika showed no emotion. He wedged the pearl-handled Colt under his belt, pointed the rifle at the ground, and fired two quick shots, which echoed off the high slopes like so much thunder.

Fargo tried another smile. "What are you doing here, anyway? And with a bunch of cows? Is there a ranch nearby I don't know about?"

"Cud Sten will ask the questions. He'll be here shortly."

Fargo wore his best poker face. He was in for it unless they believed him.

His nerves tingling, he heard riders approach. Soon they were all there, ringing him, their revolvers out and cocked.

Cud Sten hadn't drawn his. He reined up next to Rika and listened to a brief recital of Fargo's account. Then Cud fixed his dark eyes on Fargo.

"That's your story, is it, mister?"

Fargo nodded.

"It could be you're telling the truth. Then again, it could be you're an egg-sucking bastard. And if you killed my pard to get his horse and gun, you'll die in more pain than you can imagine."

"I've never stolen a horse in my life," Fargo said. "If I'd know your ranch was nearby, I'd have guessed the man rode for you and gone there to tell you I found him."

"My ranch?" Cud said, and glanced at Rika.

"The cows," Rika said.

That seemed to amuse Cud Sten. "So you reckon I'm a rancher, huh? Do you hear that, boys?"

Some of the others laughed.

"Why else would you be herding cows in all this snow?" Fargo feigned ignorance.

"Makes you wonder," Cud said.

"I'd be obliged if I could stay a night or two to rest up. As for this horse, I'll pay for him, or another if you have one to spare."

Cud's interest perked and he leaned forward. "Have a lot of money on you, do you?"

"Hardly any," Fargo said. The money that they had taken from Tull was wrapped up in his saddlebags. "You'd have to sell it to me cheap."

The redhead gigged his mount closer and wagged his six-shooter. "I don't believe a word this coyote says. I say we blast him and be on our way."

Cud Sten's features hardened. "Are you the boss now, Lear? Are you giving orders now?"

The redhead blanched. "No, Cud! Never. Not me. I wouldn't ever do that. I'm just saying, is all."

For a few seconds all eyes were on Sten as if they expected an explosion of violence.

"Is that a fact?"

"Please, Cud. I've been with you a long time. You know me."

Cud Sten smiled, and the others visibly relaxed. "I'll let it pass this time. But only because I'm in a good mood."

"Lucky devil," one of the others said.

Cud turned to Fargo. "I don't rightly know what to do with you yet, so I'm taking you with me until I do. If it turns out you're lying, I'll do things to you that would make an Apache green with envy. If you have any objections, let me hear them."

Fargo starred at the ring of hard faces and the ring of revolver muzzles, and he did the only thing he could under the circumstances. He smiled and spread his hands. "Where are we headed?"

12

Fargo's luck wasn't all bad. They didn't tie him or search him. Two did ride on either side of him, their hands on their six-shooters. Rika was up ahead, the rest behind with the cows.

One of those guarding him was Lear, and Fargo tried to strike up a conversation.

"You don't like strangers much, I take it?"

"I don't like anybody. So shut the hell up."

When Rika came to the tracks Fargo had discovered earlier, he drew rein. Cud Sten rode up and asked why Rika had stopped.

"Another shod horse," Rika said, pointing at the hoof prints. "Not Tull's. It went that way." He pointed across the grassy flatland.

"*Another* white man hereabouts?" Cud Sten rubbed his club on his chin. "The Beartooths are right popular all of a sudden. It can't be the gent we stole these cows from. We lost him and his hands days ago. Can't be a lawman, either. The law never comes this far in."

"Want me to have a look-see?"

"Of course. We'll be at the cabin. Bring him back breathing. Maybe he's a pard of simpleton here." Cud waved his club at Fargo. "If so, they'll have a heap of explaining to do."

Rika nodded and trotted toward the far trees.

Cud rose in the stirrups and bellowed at the men tending the cows, "Keep 'em moving. I aim to reach her place before dark. If we don't, it will rile me, and you don't want me riled."

Fargo clucked to the sorrel and brought it up next to Sten's animal. Neither Lear nor the other guard tried to stop him. "Mind if we talk?"

Cud regarded him with a mix of contempt and curiosity. "What's on your mind, simpleton?"

"What do you aim to do with me?"

"I've already done told you. I don't rightly know. Could be you're just passing through—in which case maybe I'll let you live. Could be you told me a pack of lies—in which case I'll break every bone in your body before I pound your skull in."

Fargo nodded at the club. "I don't see many of those."

"They're right handy." Grinning, Cud smacked the club against the palm of his other hand. "As quiet as a knife and better than a pair of fists." He patted the club.

"How'd you come to use one?"

"The first time was in a saloon fight. I busted a chair over a fella's head and it broke. He had some friends, and I took a chair leg to them. I liked it so much, I had this made." Cud fondled the thick end of the club. "Can't tell you how many heads I've split open." He gave Fargo a meaningful look.

"I heard you mention a cabin. Is that where you're taking me?"

"A lady friend of mine lives there. If you know what's good for you, you won't go anywhere near her. I've got plans for that little lady."

"To be hitched?"

"Hell, simpleton, I ain't the marrying kind. No, me and her are going to live in sin, as church folk say."

"The lady likes that idea, does she?"

"Whether she does or she doesn't, she don't have a say." Cud licked his thick lips. "I've been after this filly for a long time now and she keeps putting me off. But not anymore.

90

This time I'm having my way." He stopped and scowled. "Why the hell am I telling you this? I don't know you from Adam. Go back with the cows and don't pester me."

"One more thing," Fargo said.

Cud swore and swung the club.

Fargo tried to dodge but he couldn't pull far enough back. The club caught him on the shoulder and sent pain shooting through clear down to his toes. His boot came out of the stirrup and he was nearly unhorsed. Clinging to the saddle horn with his other hand, he managed to pull himself back up.

Sten's men were hooting and laughing.

"That'll learn you," Cud growled. "When I tell you to do something, you damn well do it. Get back with the cows, and don't let out a peep or you'll lose some teeth."

Fargo had no choice. Lear and the other man went with him, Lear chortling in sadistic glee.

The ride to the valley took an eternity. Fargo was afraid that when they got to the cabin Mary and the kids would rush out to greet him and Cud Sten would realize everything he had said was a lie. He wanted to try for the forest but he would be shot dead before he reached it. In a mental funk, he didn't look around when one of the men yelled.

Cud Sten drew rein and twisted in the saddle. "Well, will you look at that? Today is full of surprises."

Fargo stopped and turned.

Rika was trotting toward them, leading the Ovaro by the reins. The saddle was still on but it had shifted, and the Henry rifle was no longer in the scabbard. Rika was holding it.

"Any trouble?" Cud asked.

"The horse was by itself," Rika revealed. "It's worn-out and hungry. Must have been wandering for days."

"And the gent who owns it?"

Fargo said, "That would be me."

All of them looked at him.

"I told you I lost my horse in the blizzard, remember? I was worried I'd lost him for good. Now you can have your friend's horse back and I'll take mine and be on my way."

"Like hell you will," Cud said. He kneed his mount over to the Ovaro and patted the stallion's neck. "This here is one fine animal. I might take a notion to keep him for myself."

"He's mine," Rika said.

To Fargo's surprise, Cud Sten didn't object. "That's my rifle you're holding," he mentioned.

"It's mine, too." Rika trained the Henry on him. "You're welcome to try and take it back."

Some of the others laughed.

Fargo simmered but did nothing. What *could* he do when it was seven to one and all he had was a knife?

"Besides," Cud said, "how do we know they're really yours? They could belong to anybody."

Rika had let go of the Ovaro's reins, and just then the Ovaro came over to Fargo and nuzzled his leg. He rubbed its neck. "There, there, big fella. I've missed you, too." He grinned at Cud.

"Don't make a lick of difference. What we want, we take. Throw a rope over him, Rika, and bring him along."

The sun was low to the horizon when they neared the stand that hid the cabin. Smoke from the chimney coiled above the trees like a gray snake.

Fargo braced for the worst. He promised himself that before he went down, he would bury the toothpick in Cud Sten. With their leader dead, the others might leave Mary be.

They wound through the trees and drew rein. The curtain over the window moved. Then the door opened and Mary came out, her arms around Nelly and Jayce. "Mr. Sten," she said formally.

Fargo saw Jayce spot him and open his mouth but Mary's fingers tightened on the boy's shoulder and she whispered something. Jayce closed his mouth and looked away.

"It's great to see you again, Mary gal," Cud Sten blustered. "There hasn't been a day gone by that I haven't thought of you."

"It must be my cooking."

Cud laughed a lot louder than her quip called for. Alighting, he motioned with his club at the cows. "I brought you presents, gal. Six of them. You're always saying as how you never have enough to eat. Now you'll have plenty of milk for the sprouts. And if you want, my men will butcher one of these critters and smoke and dry the meat so you have enough to last you the whole winter." Cud beamed at his own generosity. "How does that sound?"

"I can't accept gifts from you, Mr. Sten."

"Of course you can. We're friends, ain't we? And what are friends for if not to help one another out?"

Rika said, "Ask her about Tull."

Cud glanced at him in some annoyance, but then said, "Got a question for you, Mary gal. I sent my man Tull on ahead to make sure you were all right. Did he ever show?"

"I haven't seen Mr. Tull since the last time you paid us a visit."

Cud fixed on her face, trying to read by her expression if she was telling the truth.

Fargo had to hand it to her; Mary would make a great poker player. Nelly, though, averted her gaze and nervously shifted her weight from one foot to the other. Fargo couldn't tell if Cud noticed.

Mary turned innocent eyes on him. "Isn't this man riding Mr. Tull's horse?"

"He sure is. He says he found Tull with an arrow in him and had to help himself to Tull's because he lost his own."

Mary gazed at the Ovaro. "And who does this fine animal belong to?"

"We found it along the way and Rika has taken a shine to him. But if you ask real nice, Rika might let you ride him."

"I refuse to ask any favors of Mr. Rika."

"Now, now, what has he ever done to you?" Cud smiled his warmest smile. "Enough of this standing around in the cold." He pointed his club at Lear and another man. "You two see to the beeves. Put them in the corral. Since there ain't room for the cows and our horses both, you'll have to picket the horses. Tie the rope good and tight. If any of the horses get loose, I'll have your hides. Bring our gear when you come in. The rest of you boys can come inside now." He looked at Fargo. "You, too, stranger."

The warmth of the cabin was a welcome relief. Fargo went over and sat on the floor by the fireplace, his legs bent, his hands close to the tops of his boots so he could get to the Arkansas toothpick quickly if he had to.

Cud and his men took seats at the table. Not Rika, though; he stood in a corner, the Henry cradled in his arms, as motionless as a statue.

Mary sent Nelly and Jayce into their room and told them to close the door. She stepped to the stove and put coffee on. "This is the last I have. I'm afraid you'll have to do without once this is gone."

"That's what you think" Cud responded. "I brought you a bunch of vittles. Coffee. A bag of flour. Sugar. I even brought some of those lemon drops your sprouts like."

"You spoil me," Mary said drily.

"And you know why."

"Please, Mr. Sten, I've asked you before not to make more of our relationship than there can ever possibly be. I haven't been a widow all that long. I need more time to heal."

"It's been pretty near a year," Cud growled. "If you ain't healed by now, you ain't never going to be." He forced a smile. "What you need is another man so you can forget about— What was his name?"

"Frank," Mary said softly.

"So you can forget about Frank and get on with your life.

You need a man who doesn't mind coming all this way to be with you. A man who brings you gifts and treats your sprouts decent."

"They're children, Mr. Sten, not plants. And you are referring to yourself, I take it."

"I've made my interest plain. I've been awful patient with you because you're special. But my patience has about run out. You need to make up your mind and you need to do it soon."

Fargo caught the implied threat. So, too, he suspected, did Mary, but she didn't let on.

When Lear and the other man came in with the saddle-bags and bedrolls, Cud made a show of giving her the food he had brought.

"Whip us up some supper, why don't you? I sure am hungry. In fact, I'll have my men butcher one of the cows right this minute so we can have thick, juicy steaks. How would that be?"

"I don't mind cooking for you," Mary said in a tone that suggested she minded very much.

"Ain't you a peach!" Cud barked orders for two of his men to do the butchering. He sat like some king holding court, and declared, "Yes, sir. This is the life. A roof over my head, a fine gal to cook a good meal, and my pards for company. What more can a man ask for?"

"I never took you for a homebody," Lear said.

"You don't know me very well. None of you do. I've got the same hankerings as most any man. I won't do what I'm doing forever. One day I'll want to hang up my six-gun and sit in a rocking chair and take life easy." Cud gazed expansively about the room. "I can't think of a better place to live out my days than right here."

Fargo could guess why. There wasn't any law for hundreds of miles. Plus, it was so deep into the Beartooth Mountains, no one would think to look for Cud there.

"How about a game?" a man suggested.

Cards were produced. Poker hands were dealt.

Fargo would have loved to sit in, but he wasn't asked. The outlaws were ignoring him, which suited him fine.

Coincidentally, just then Cud glanced around. "Don't think I've forgotten about you, mister. I haven't. After I've eaten and relaxed a spell, I'll make up my mind what to do with you."

Mary heard, and asked, "What do mean, Mr. Sten? What is it you have to decide?"

"Whether simpleton here lives or dies."

13

Out behind the cabin a cow commenced to squall and low in terror and pain. The men sent to do the butchering were doing a poor job. It was supposed to be quick: Slit the cow's throat so the cow bled out fast, and down it went. Either they didn't cut deep enough or they were trying some other way, and the cow was in torment.

Nelly and Jayce ran out of their room, Nelly crying. "Ma? What are those awful sounds?"

"It's all right," Mary assured them, and gave Cud Sten a look that would blister paint.

Cud put down his cards. Standing up, he hitched at his gun belt. "I'm sorry, gal. I've got me a bunch of idiots who can't do nothing right." He started toward the door, saw Rika in the corner, and added, "Except for you." He slammed the front door after him. Not ten seconds later the blast of a revolver put an end to the squalling.

Fargo noticed that the men at the table appeared nervous. Apparently riding with Cud Sten was like riding with a rabid wolf: They never knew but when the wolf would turn on them.

Cud opened the front door and took a step inside.

"Your boots, Mr. Sten," Mary said.

"What about them?"

"You'll track snow in. Clean them off, if you please."

Cud looked down at his snow-caked boots and then at her. "You mean it?"

"This is my home. I like to keep it clean."

"Hell, gal," Cud said. But he kicked his boots against the outer wall until most of the snow was off. "How's that?"

"You're a perfect gentleman."

Beaming, Cud went over to his chair. "Did you hear her, boys? No one's ever called me that before."

"I wonder why," one of them muttered.

Cud cuffed him.

Fargo was debating what to do. He took Cud's threat seriously. The man wouldn't think twice about killing him. The smart thing was to get out of there but that meant deserting Mary and her kids.

Cud produced a flask. He drank, then smacked his lips and set the flask on the table with a loud *thunk*. "That sure hit the spot."

Mary was mixing ingredients in a baking pan. She swiped at a bang, leaving a line of flour across her forehead, and said, "What have I told you about liquor, Mr. Sten?"

"A man has to have a nip now and then."

"My Frank refrained. I expect you to do the same when you are under my roof. For the children's sake."

Cud Sten scowled. "You're beginning to annoy me, gal. One minute I'm a gent. The next you are on me about my drinking."

"Ain't that just like a female?" blurted the man who been cuffed. He recoiled, expecting another blow, but Cud was glaring at Mary.

"We need to get a few things straight, gal. I'm willing to bend my ways to suit you, but only to a point. I won't stop drinking whiskey on account of you don't like it."

"Then you won't be welcome under my roof anymore."

Cud half came out of his chair. Fargo tensed to move between them, but Cud sat back down and grumbled.

"You seem to forget I'm a lady, Mr. Sten. Perhaps you

have become so accustomed to women of loose morals that you think all women are the same. I assure you we're not."

"Wait a minute. Are you saying that if I mend my ways, you'll think more highly of me?"

"How could I not?"

The veiled insult was lost on Cud, who grinned and declared, "Well, now, if that's the case, I reckon I can be as much of a gentleman as simpleton over there." He fixed his dark eyes on Fargo. "Why don't you come over and join us, simpleton?"

"Be glad to." Fargo sat in an empty chair across from Sten so he would have a split-second warning if Sten went for his revolver. "There's nothing I like better than whiskey and a good game of cards." He reached for the flask but Cud snatched it from the table.

"I don't share my coffin varnish with anybody." Cud capped the flask and shoved it into a pocket. "I didn't ask you over to drink nor take a hand, neither. It's time."

"For what?" Fargo played his part.

"To decide what I'm going to do with you." Cud's thick brows pinched together and he drummed on the table. "It appears you were telling the truth about Tull. The damn Injuns got him."

The others at the table showed little interest. One man was picking his teeth with a card.

Fargo moved his head just enough to see Rika over in the corner. Rika held the Henry trained on his back. All it was take was a nod from Cud Sten, and Rika would blow a hole in him. "Does this mean I can have my horse and my effects and be on my way?"

"The horse is Rika's now. The sooner you get used to that notion, the better off you'll be." Cud paused. "I haven't seen many like it. It's not an Appaloosa and it's not a pinto."

"It's a kind of pinto," Fargo educated him. "Some folks

call it an Ovaro." The markings told the difference; the dark spots on the Ovaro were smaller than on most pintos, and there were more of them.

"Ovaro," Cud rolled the word on his tongue. "It has a fancy sound, don't you think?"

"I think Rika should pay for him."

Cud Sten blinked and half his men either laughed or looked at Fargo as if he were five bales short of a wagonload. "What did you just say?"

"It's not right that your friend just takes him. Rika should pay me for my horse. That's only fair."

"Why should he pay for it when it's already his?" Cud did more finger-drumming, and a slow smirk spread across his face. "But I'll tell you what I'll do. You can make this easy, or you can make it hard, but I don't think you'll like hard."

"What's your idea of easy?"

"I let you keep Tull's horse and you go on breathing. His for yours. I call that a fair trade."

"And my rifle and the pearl-handled Colt?"

"That Colt was never yours to begin with so you don't have a claim. The rifle, well—" Cud nodded at Rika.

Fargo held his anger in check. There was a time and a place for anger, and this wasn't it. But he did say, "That's your notion of fair?"

"You keep missing the important part," Cud Sten said. "Or doesn't it matter to you whether you breathe air or dirt?"

There it was: Either Fargo agreed or they killed him and if he did agree, they might kill him later, anyway. He tested his suspicion. "Let's say I agree. Can I saddle up and head out right this minute?"

"What's your hurry? It'll be dark soon. You should stick around, have some of my Mary's cooking, and get a good night's rest."

Fargo saw Mary's back go rigid and her hand clench a

wood spoon until her knuckles were pale. She didn't like that "my Mary." "You must want me dead."

"Why do you say that?"

"Sending me off unarmed. I'll end up like your friend Tull."

"Those Injuns are probably long gone. But I'll tell you what I'll do. I'll keep Tull's pearl-handled Colt for myself and give you my revolver. How would that be?"

Before Fargo could answer, the front door opened and in came the pair who had butchered the cow. Their clothes were spattered with blood and gore caked their hands. They were carrying thick slabs of meat, which they brought to the table, dripping blood with every step.

"Here're those steaks you wanted, Cud."

"I can see that, Howell. But what I don't get is why you're making a mess of my gal's floor."

"What?" Howell glanced down. "Is she going to fuss over a little blood?"

Cud stabbed a finger at them. "Put the meat on the counter and clean the floor on your way back. Then get to work smoking the rest of the meat."

"We don't have that cow half cut up yet. It could take us until midnight."

"So? We're not going anywhere. I'll call you when it's time to eat." Cud looked at Mary, evidently thinking he deserved a compliment of some kind, but she had her back to them. Cud turned to Fargo. "Now, then, where were we?"

"You were saying as how you're going to give my rifle back and let me saddle my Ovaro and light a shuck."

"You don't give up, do you? It's Tull's horse and my revolver, or it's nothing. Which will it be?"

"You don't leave me much choice."

"I don't leave you none."

Fargo was a bit surprised that Sten hadn't tried to blow

out his wick. Now that Sten had learned the truth about Tull, or thought he had, there was no reason for Sten to keep him alive. Fargo figured Mary must have something to do with it; Cud was trying to impress her by not killing him.

The dealer began shuffling the cards.

"Deal me in," Fargo said, and jerked a thumb at where Rika still stood over in the corner. "How about your friend? Does he want to join us?"

"What the hell do you care? He does what he wants. Unlike these other lunkheads, I can always count on him to do what's best."

Lear glared at Fargo. "I don't like this varmint much. I get the notion he's a tricky son of a bitch."

From over at the stove Mary said, "Mr. Lear, your language, please."

"Oh, hell."

"That's exactly what I mean."

Lear switched his glare to Cud Sten. "How much longer do we have to put up with her? This ain't a church social, for God's sake."

"You'll treat her nice and like it," Cud said flatly, and placed his hand on his club.

"Oh, hell," Lear said again.

Fargo considered the cards he was dealt. "I have an idea," he announced.

"Not another one," Cud said.

"How about if we play a hand with my horse and rifle as the stake? I win, I get them back."

"Mister, you plumb amaze me. When you gnaw on a bone, you don't let up. What makes you think I'd gamble for them when we already have them?"

Fargo decided to put his immunity to the test. "I just thought you might want to show Mrs. Harper that you're not as big a bastard as everyone says you are."

Everyone at the table froze.

That included Cud Sten. His face resembled stone. But then, ever so slowly, his features shifted until they mirrored pure, vicious hate. "No one talks to me like that."

Mary picked that moment to come over carrying the coffeepot and several cups. "I don't have enough for everyone, so you'll have to use some of your own." She set a cup next to Cud and began filling it.

Sten was struggling to control himself. His face twitched, his mouth worked, and his jaw muscles bulged.

"Cat got your tongue?" Mary asked.

"No, ma'am," Cud said harshly. "It's him. You didn't hear what he just said to me."

"Oh, I heard," Mary said sweetly. "I've heard everything. And I'm appalled, Mr. Sten. You steal from him and act like you're doing him a favor. Here I thought you were trying to show me how much of a gentleman you could be."

Cud's eyes were twin daggers. "You can't expect me not to be me. It doesn't work like that."

"All I know is that I couldn't like a man who lords it over other folks. I'm disappointed. Here we were starting to be friends, too." Mary turned and placed a cup in front of Fargo and began pouring.

Cud Sten's whole body seemed to swell with rage but gradually the fury drained away and a cold smile replaced his bloodlust. "I don't want you thinking poorly of me, gal. So I'll tell you what I'll do. I'll gamble for them like he wants. How would that be?"

"You would do that? For me?"

Cud was like a puppy that had been patted on the head. "All I care about is pleasing you."

"See? You can be nice when you try." Mary set the pot down. "Help yourselves. I have to finish supper."

Cud watched her, and when she was over at the counter, he leaned toward Fargo and said so she couldn't hear, "Your horse and rifle ain't all you're playing for, you rotten son of a

103

btich." Sitting back, he smiled and said, "Now, then, how many cards do you want?"

Fargo had two kings, two twos, and a ten. Another king or another two and he would have a full house. The odds were high against drawing either, but even if he didn't, he'd still have two pair. He discarded the ten. "I'll take one."

"I'll stick with these." Cud dealt a card from the top of the deck and slid it across.

Covering it with his hand, Fargo peeked. It was a queen. Of no use to him whatsoever.

"What do you have?" Fargo flipped his cards over. "Two pair, kings and twos."

"Ain't that a shame." Cud Sten slowly turned his cards over. "I've got me a straight. You lose, mister. You lose big."

14

"You have to escape. He's going to kill you," Mary whispered to Fargo when she brought his plate.

He was seated by the fireplace, his back to the wall, his knees drawn to his chest. "I know."

Cud Sten kept staring over at him, always with the same cold grin, a cat playing with a mouse.

"Why did you bait him like that?" Mary whispered. "If you'd kept quiet, maybe he would have let you live."

"Who's fooling who?" Fargo never doubted for a moment that Sten intended to turn him into maggot bait.

"What can I do to help?"

"Nothing." Fargo didn't want her to be part of it. He didn't want her hurt. Cud Sten might easily turn on her if she got him mad enough.

Mary straightened. Her eyes were moist and she had to swallow to say, "I can't just stand by and let that beast murder you. Not after we—" She couldn't finish.

"It's not just me you have to think of," Fargo reminded her.

"We're in this together. They want to help, too."

From the table came an angry bellow. "What are you two whispering about over there? Mary, gal, you shouldn't have anything to do with him. I don't like him much."

Mary wheeled. "I'll choose my own friends, Mr. Sten, thank you very much."

The vehemence in her voice made Cud sit up. "Now, now, don't get all female on me."

Fargo marveled at Mary's self-control. Her spine ramrod stiff, she marched to the stove and put two plates on a tray. "I'm taking these to Nelly and Jayce."

"They're welcome to join us at the table," Cud said. "I like your sprouts. That girl of yours is almost as pretty as you."

Mary glanced at Sten and Fargo saw a new fear creep into her eyes. But she smothered it, crossed to their bedroom, knocked, and went in.

No sooner did the door close behind her than Cud Sten was out of his chair, his club in his right hand. The others rose, too, their hands on their hardware. Over in the corner, Rika raised the Henry to his shoulder.

About to cut a piece of steak, Fargo grinned. "Looks like I won, after all."

Halfway to the hearth, Cud stopped in puzzlement. "Won what?"

"I bet myself you couldn't wait until she goes to bed to do it. You and her boy are about the same age."

"Are you loco? I'm a grown man." Cud wagged his club. "On your feet. You're going to the outhouse."

"I am?"

Cud took another step. "Don't make me do it here. She won't like having your brains smeared all over her floor."

"Easy, now," Fargo said, rising. He would wait until they got him outside. It was safer for the Harpers that way.

Keeping his voice low, Cud turned to Lear. "You and Charlie take him out. Tie him and gag him and stick him in the woodshed."

"You're not going to kill him?"

"Of course I am, you stupid son of a bitch. But I want to do it nice and slow. I'll wait until the gal and her sprouts are asleep."

Lear drew his six-shooter. "Let's go, mister."

Fargo held his hands up and moved toward the door. The skin on his back prickled as he passed Cud Sten. He half expected Sten to club him. He took another step, and suddenly his head exploded with pain. His legs gave out and he clutched at a chair to stay on his feet but missed. Rough hands grabbed his arms. He heard laughter, and then he was sucked into blackness.

The cold revived him.

Fargo opened his eyes and groaned. His head felt as if it had been split open. He was lying on his side, his wrists and ankles tied tight. He was in a cramped space. That much he could tell. He smelled musty earth under his cheek. Groggily, he tried to raise his head and nearly passed out.

Fargo remembered something being said about the woodshed. He'd ridden past it a few times and not paid much attention; it was on the side of the cabin, enclosed on three sides, with pine boughs for a roof. Only about waist-high, it was maybe five feet from end to end.

Gradually his eyes adjusted. Firewood was stacked in front of him. He extended his arms as far back as he could and touched snow, which explained why his back was colder than his front. Clenching his teeth, he twisted his head. All he saw was snow-shrouded trees.

He pried at the rope around his ankles. The knots were iron.

From inside the cabin came gruff mirth.

Suddenly Fargo remembered something else: Cud Sten was going to wait until Mary and the children turned in, then come out and beat him to death. Well, he would have a surprise for the bastard. Shifting his shoulder, he hiked at his pant leg and got it high enough to slide his fingers into his boot. For a few seconds he thought he had the wrong boot; the Arkansas toothpick wasn't there. Then he felt the ankle sheath, and the terrible truth dawned. They had found the toothpick and taken it.

A new cold spread through Fargo, a cold that had nothing to do with the temperature. He tried to recall if he had seen an ax anywhere near the woodshed or anything else sharp lying around that he could use to cut himself free.

Fargo wondered what time it was. Mary wouldn't stay up late. Any minute now Sten might come out to kill him. Fighting off waves of pain, he tried to roll over. He had to try twice to do it, and then he lay grimacing, his stomach queasy. One of the wolf bites was hurting, too.

One of the wolf bites.

Fargo sat up. He had an idea. Not much of one, but he was desperate, and desperate men grasped at straws. His straw lay down the valley. Hunching his shoulders, he got to his knees.

Now came the hard part. Fargo inched forward, moving first one knee and then the other. Once he was out from under the pine boughs, he lurched upright—and fell on his face in the snow. Spitting, he made it back to his knees.

"You can do this."

Fargo heaved erect. Again he teetered but he kept his balance. He began to hop. By bending forward he was able to keep his balance. He made it to the pines and paused to catch his breath and get his bearings. Then he was off again, hopping like an oversized jackrabbit. He had to be careful and not try to hop too far and be sure to land with both boots flat. It was slow going at first. But the more he did it, the better he got; when he emerged from the trees, he was moving faster than he thought he could.

There was no moon. Pale starlight dulled the white of the snow so that it was almost brown.

Fargo hopped and hopped. He had a fair idea where to find what he was looking for, but it would take time to get there. The question was, how much did he have? How soon before Cud Sten discovered he was gone and the outlaws came looking for him?

To the north a lonesome coyote yipped. Up on the mountain an owl hooted.

Fargo hoped he didn't run into more starved wolves or a hungry bear. Given how his luck had been running, he wouldn't be surprised if either happened.

He shut everything from his mind and concentrated on hopping. His leg muscles protested but the pain in his legs was nothing compared to the throbbing in his head. Hunch, jump, land. Hunch, jump, land. He settled into a rhythm. Once, when he glanced back to see if anyone was after him, he was surprised at how far he had gone.

Fargo wondered if he would find it. He didn't think it was that far, but he had been fading in and out of consciousness when they'd hauled him to the cabin, and maybe his memory of things wasn't as it was.

He wondered, too, if maybe there was a better way, a smarter way. Maybe the knock on the head had jumbled it so bad he wasn't thinking right.

The pain brought him to a stop. He needed to rest a minute. He looked back again. Was it his imagination or did he hear voices?

He definitely heard a footstep close by, the crunch of the snow as something moved toward him out of the dark. He tensed, dreading that the vague shape he discerned was a grizzly. He was helpless—totally helpless. All he would be able to do was scream, and he would be damned if he would do that.

The shape grew larger. It was easily as tall as a griz. But the proportions were wrong. He almost laughed when he recognized what it was.

It was curious. It came within a few yards and sniffed, trying to tell exactly what he was. Then it knew, and it snorted and raised its head and stamped, and suddenly he wasn't as safe as he thought he was.

The bull elk stamped again. Its antlers were barely visible

but they were long and sharp and formidable enough that if the elk decided to charge, it could gore him to death.

Fargo once heard of a hunter killed by an elk when the man walked up to it without making sure it was dead. Another man kept penned elk in a corral and sold elk meat at a good prices until one morning he walked into the corral to feed them and one of the bulls wanted out and went through him to escape.

So now Fargo froze and waited for the bull elk to make up its mind. It lowered its head and shook it. He braced for the worst but the elk swung away and went on by, snorting and blowing clouds of breath. He didn't do anything or say anything and watched until it was out of sight.

Fargo resumed hopping. He cast about for a dark spot on the snow. It was in the open so it should be easy to spot. Then he realized the snow had done a lot of drifting since he was attacked. It could be the remains were covered and he wouldn't find them. In which case, come daylight, Cud Sten would find him, and that would be that.

He looked back again and saw balls of fire moving about near the cabin. Torches. They had discovered he was missing and they were looking for him. His tracks would be easy to find. Soon they would mount up and come after him.

"Damn," Fargo said out loud. He hopped to the right and then to the left. He went another ten yards, his frustration mounting.

Then, of a sudden, there it was, a dark patch of fur-covered bones. Most of the wolf was gone. The buzzards and coyotes and other scavengers had been at it. In another week there wouldn't be anything left except for a few bones that hadn't been gnawed down to the marrow or dragged off.

The thought chilled him. What if something had dragged off the head? He plopped down on his knees and bent low. The reek wasn't as awful as it would be if it were summer but it was awful enough. He held his breath and bent lower and there it was, the skull, stripped of eyes and ears and tongues and almost all the fur. The part Fargo was interested in—the jaw—was intact.

Fargo turned so his back and his bound hands were toward the skull. Looking over his shoulder, he gripped the lower jaw and sought to pry it wider so there was room for his wrists. The bone refused to move. It was locked fast, or frozen.

He tried again, worried he might snap it. It moved, but only a little. That would have to do.

The balls of fire had left the vicinity of the cabin and were spreading out among the pines.

Fargo shoved his wrists between the razor teeth. He rubbed back and forth, sawing. It hurt his shoulders. His arms began to ache. He kept at it, counting on the rope to give before he did. He had the best of incentives: Men were out to kill him.

He accidentally brushed his wrist against teeth and winced when they dug into his flesh. From then on he was extra careful but he couldn't help scraping and nicking himself. It was slow going. Unfortunately, he didn't have a minute to spare.

The torches were converging on the rear of the cabin, on the corral. The outlaws were about to throw saddles on their horses and come after him.

Fargo sawed harder. If he cut himself that was too bad. The important thing was to live.

A shot cracked from the vicinity of the cabin.

Fargo looked up in surprise. He couldn't think of why anyone would shoot. The torches were moving every which way. There was some sort of commotion. He speculated it was a signal.

Then another possibility occurred to him and turned him colder than the temperature. It made the best sense and spelled trouble for Mary and her children.

Someone was shouting. Cud Sten, it sounded like. The wind carried his voice clear.

"Take her inside and keep her there! And make sure those kids stay in their bedroom!"

Fargo swore. Mary must have tried to stop them.

He wrapped his wrists around the lower jaw. There was more give in the rope. He strained but it refused to cut all the way through. Or at least to where he could break it.

Two of the torches were higher off the ground than the rest, and they were coming in his direction. It meant two of the outlaws were on horseback, and tracking him.

"Damn it."

Fargo sawed faster. He was beginning to doubt it would ever work—when it did. His forearms and his hands were loose. They hurt. God, they hurt. But he was free.

Gripping the bottom jaw, Fargo wrenched with all his might, breaking it off. He turned and swung his legs in front of him. Pressing hard, he cut at the rope. It went faster now but not fast enough to suit him. Finally, it was done. He went to push to his feet.

He had run out of time.

Hooves pounded the snow.

Fargo looked up.

The starlight lent a spectral cast to the pair of riders who were almost on top of him.

15

The torches had yet to catch Skye Fargo in their glow. Whirling, he ran a dozen long strides and threw himself flat. He still held the jawbone.

The two outlaws were almost to the wolf when they spotted it. They slowed, and gun metal gleamed.

"What the hell is that?" Lear snapped.

"Looks like a dead animal to me," the other rider said. He drew rein and swung down. Dropping to one knee, he declared, "Yep. It's a dead wolf." He scoured the snow around it. "From the look of things, the hombre we're after knelt here a while."

"What the hell for?"

The other man shrugged. "Your guess is as good as mine. Maybe he was hungry."

"There's not anything left of that wolf to eat," Lear observed. "Get back on your horse, Boyce. We'll keep searching. He can't be that far ahead."

Boyce unfurled and turned to his mount. Lear was gazing into the night.

Fargo would never have a better chance. Leaping to his feet, he rushed them, his legs flying.

"Look out!" Lear bawled.

Boyce spun and brought up his six-shooter.

But Fargo was close enough that all he had to do was swing the jawbone in a short arc. The teeth ripped across Boyce's throat. Blood spurted, and Boyce shrieked and stumbled back, frantically pressing his other hand to the wound in a vain bid to stanch the flow. He banged off a shot that missed.

Fargo hadn't slowed; he veered toward Lear. Lear fired, but in his fear and his haste, he missed.

Taking a last running step, Fargo launched himself into the air. He hooked one arm around Lear's waist even as he slashed at Lear's face. Then they were falling. So was the torch. Lear cursed when he hit.

Fargo was up in a twinkling, and he sprang. He cut at Lear's gun hand and drew more blood; the revolver fell to the snow.

Lear bleated and scrambled back.

Fargo went after him. He avoided a bootheel to the knee and was coiling to spring when a battering ram slammed into his back and threw him to his hands and knees. He twisted, and a knife flashed past his face.

"I'll kill you, bastard!" Boyce raged. "Kill you dead!"

Fargo was amazed the man had life left. The wolf jaw had done a good job; the cut, which was half an inch deep, gushed blood.

Boyce thrust at Fargo's heart. Lightning swift, Fargo seized the man's arm and jacked his knee into the elbow. The *crunch* was sickeningly loud. Boyce threw back his head and screeched, and Fargo raked the jawbone across his throat a second time.

Hooves drummed.

Thinking it was more of Sten's men, Fargo spun. But it was Lear, back in the saddle and fleeing toward the cabin. The man had all the backbone of a soggy slice of bread.

Terrible gurgling sounds issued from Boyce's ravaged throat. He had fallen and was kicking and twitching. Gamely he sought to cover the wounds but blood spewed between his fingers. He arched his back, his mouth parted, and he uttered a last strangled cry. Then he went limp.

Fargo had no time to lose. He threw the jawbone away and groped for the man's six-gun. A hole in the snow seemed a likely spot. He plunged his hands in and brought them out holding a long-barreled Remington. It wouldn't fit in his holster, so he swiftly unbuckled Boyce's gun belt, jammed the revolver into the holster, and rose.

Boyce's horse, a small dun, had gone a short way and stopped. Its head was up and its nostrils flared. The violence and the scent of blood had it poised to bolt.

"Easy, boy, easy." Walking slowly toward it, Fargo held out his hand. He let it sniff him, then patted its neck. "See? I'm as friendly as he can be." He went on talking softly and soothingly as he gripped the saddle horn and raised his boot to the stirrup.

Another moment, and Fargo was in the saddle. He strapped Boyce's gun belt around his waist so the holster was on his left side, the Remington butt-forward. His own holster was on the right.

Now he had riding to do. He lifted the reins and paused. The fading light from the sputtering torch bathed Boyce's pale face, ringed by bright scarlet

Lear was shouting up a storm.

Fargo reined toward the mountains to the north. He figured Sten's entire gang would be after him. In fact, he was counting on it. He rode hard. Although smaller than the Ovaro, the dun made up in vitality what it lacked in size and plowed through the snow as neatly as a knife. When he had gone about a hundred yards, he reined toward the trees that sheltered the cabin.

Red and orange fireflies were coming the other way, heading for the dead wolf. Every rider save one had a torch; the one without was probably Lear. Cud Sten was in the lead, holding both a torch and his club.

Fargo slowed and bent low over the saddle. He wasn't taking any chances. When the outlaws were well past, he straightened and jabbed his spurs. The dun seemed to delight in pushing itself.

The glow of the cabin window served as a beacon.

Fargo slowed again when he reached the trees. He reined to the rear, hoping against hope, and smiled when he beheld the Ovaro tied outside the corral, along with Tull's sorrel. He was off the dun before it stopped moving. There was no sign of his saddle or saddle blanket. He ran around to the front and was about to pound on the door when it was jerked open.

"Skye!"

Fargo wasn't expecting Mary to throw herself into his arms. She hugged him close, her breath warm on his neck.

"Thank God you're alive! I was so worried. I tried to stop them from going after you by grabbing a revolver, but they took it from me."

"You took an awful chance."

Past her were Nelly and Jayce, fear writ on their features.

"It won't take them long to discover I've circled around," Fargo said, hurrying inside. His saddle and saddle blanket were over against a wall. "I'll get these and be gone before they show up."

"You're taking me with you."

Fargo looked at her. "I wouldn't have it any other way."

Mary beamed.

"What about them?" Fargo demanded, with a sweep of his arm at her offspring.

"Need you even ask? Where I go, they go." Mary wrung her hands and had difficulty saying, "It's now or never. Cud is determined to have me. Before the ruckus began, he told me that he was spending the night in my bedroom. When I said that was up to me and not to him, he laughed in my face."

"You have to help her, mister," Jayce said.

"Please," Nelly begged.

"Did you think I wouldn't?" Fargo responded. "But just

so you know, not one of us might make it out of the Bear-tooths alive."

Nelly mustered a small smile. "Don't sugarcoat it. Tell us how it will really be."

"Gather up what food we can take," Fargo directed. "Bundle up warm. I'll saddle the horses." He took a step, then glanced at Nelly and Jayce. "Can you two ride?"

"They've ridden before, but not a lot," Mary answered. "Neither have I. But don't worry. We'll keep up."

Fargo got their mounts ready and brought them around to the front of the cabin. He found where the outlaws were smoking the cow meat. The strips weren't fully smoked, but they were better than empty bellies. He loaded as much as he swiftly could into saddlebags.

Mary and her children came out. They wore layers of clothes and had on coats and boots. Each had a bedroll. Mary's doing, Fargo reckoned. He tied everything on, then boosted Nelly and Jayce onto the sorrel and Mary onto the dun. She reached inside her coat.

"I have something for you. Cud Sten left it on the table when he ran out to search for you."

It was Fargo's Colt. He could have kissed her. He checked that it was loaded and twirled it into his holster. Removing the other holster with the Remington, he held them out to Mary.

"I won't be much good with it." But she hurriedly strapped it on.

That reminded Fargo. "Where's your rifle?"

"One of Sten's men took it."

Out beyond the stand, the torches were strung in a line—and that line was making for the cabin.

"Stay close." Fargo's saddle creaked under him. He reined in the opposite direction and threaded through the trees, keeping the cabin between them and the torches. Once out of the stand he had Mary come up on one side of him and the kids on the other. Together they struck out across the valley floor.

"There aren't words to thank you in," Mary said. "Most men wouldn't do what you're doing."

"No one takes my rifle and my revolver and my horse and cracks me over the head," Fargo said.

"Oh. So you're not doing this because of me? You're out for revenge."

Some folks were of the opinion Fargo was a heartless bastard. But there were a number of things he couldn't abide. One was mistreating a horse. That always got him good and mad. Another was seeing a woman or child hurt. The third was a card cheat. The fourth was any bartender who watered down his whiskey. And last—but at the top of the list—was being treated as Cud Sten had treated him. "It's more than just revenge."

"Thank you for that," Mary said. "Since my Frank died—"

"You need to get over him."

"I know. It's been a year or better. I try but I just can't. I was very much in love with him."

"Dead is dead," Fargo said.

"That was harsh. And you'd do well to remember that those we love often live on in our hearts."

Fargo looked at her. In the starlight she looked gorgeous enough to eat. "I've lost a few people who were close to me. The best thing is to close the door and get on with your life."

"I can't ever close the door to Frank. The best I can do is leave it open but only go in now and again."

She was quiet a while. Then she cleared her throat.

"Mind if I ask what your plans for us are?"

"To get you to a settlement. From there you can go anywhere you want."

"You mean never come back? But our things. We don't own much but I would like to keep what little we have."

"I didn't see a wagon anywhere."

"Frank used most of the board for firewood. He didn't ever plan to leave that place."

"Poke your head in that door and tell him he was a jackass."

On the other side of Fargo, Jayce said angrily, "Our pa was not, neither! Don't call him names."

Fargo was tempted to tell the boy that any man who brought his family out into the heart of Indian country, where there wasn't another settler within hundreds of miles, a region so remote it was crawling with predators, both four-legged and two-legged—that man was in dire need of common sense. But all he said was, "When you're older don't do as he did."

"Our pa loved us," Nelly spoke up.

"He loved you so much, he's reaching out from his grave to get you killed."

"Enough, Skye," Mary said. "They're young. They wouldn't understand. I do, and I forgive Frank his faults. For me it matters more that he was devoted to me and to them."

"Some men are good at that." Fargo doubted he was. He had too much wanderlust.

"A person never knows until they try it."

Fargo let it drop. He shifted in the saddle.

The fireflies were at the cabin.

Mary did as he was doing. "Will they come after us, you think, or wait until daylight?"

"It depends on how mad Sten is."

"He was terrible mad. He beat the man who tied you, Howell. He said Howell hadn't done it good enough. I thought for a minute Cud would beat him to death."

Jayce said, "I hate Cud Sten."

"Now, now, son."

"I do, Ma. I know you said it's not nice to hate but I can't help it. I hate him and those mean men with him. I wish they were all dead."

"Me, too," Nelly said.

A gust of wind chilled Fargo's face. It was going to be a long night. Mary and the kids would be worn-out by dawn, and the worst was yet to come.

"Oh, look!" Mary burst out. "One of them is coming after us."

A single torch was winding through the stand.

"Why only one?" Nelly wondered.

Fargo knew why. Because that one was the best tracker, and the deadliest of the bunch.

Rika was on their trail.

16

It was the middle of the morning. The air had turned bitterly cold and the cold helped Fargo stay alert. The kids, though, were dozing in the saddle, and Jayce had nearly fallen off twice.

Mary stifled a yawn. "Goodness, I'm so tired I can barely keep my eyes open."

"We can't stop yet."

They were past the point where Fargo had first spotted the outlaws. Snowy slopes climbed toward the distant sky. High above, white peaks loomed against the blue.

"There's no sign of anyone after us," Mary mentioned. "Shouldn't he have caught up by now?"

"Yes." And Fargo was beginning to worry. Rika was stalking them as a hunter stalked prey. At that very moment Rika might be in the forest, watching them.

"Why hasn't he done anything?"

"He'll pick the time and place that's best for him."

"Will he try to kill us or take us back to Sten?"

Fargo imagined it would be the latter for Mary and the kids. Him, Rika would be out to kill unless Cud Sten wanted the sadistic pleasure of killing him personally.

The sun climbed to its zenith, and Fargo called a halt. Nelly and Jayce were so tired, they shuffled to a clear spot under a pine, sat with their backs to the trunk, and fell asleep within moments.

Mary regarded them with deep love in her eyes. "They're so young. I wish they didn't have to go through this."

"Spitting into the wind."

"Sorry?"

"Wishing is like spitting into the wind."

"It's a waste of effort, in other words? Maybe so. We all of us wish for a lot in our lives that never turns out like we want it to. But that shouldn't stop a person from hoping, from wanting things to be better."

Fargo shrugged. "Taking it one day at a time makes for less disappointment."

Mary grinned. "Why, Skye Fargo, I had no idea you were a philosopher as well as the handsomest man alive."

Fargo almost reached for her. Instead he scanned the woods as he had been doing all morning.

"Do you realize that even with all that's been happening, this is the happiest I've been since Frank died?"

"I know some people," Fargo said. "A married couple. Friends of mine. He was an officer in the army and just got out after twenty years. He and his wife would understand what you've been through. They might be willing to help you resettle. I can give you a note to take to them."

Mary fixed those lovely eyes of hers on him. "You continue to surprise me in good ways."

"Don't make a big to-do out of it. He owes me. I saved him from the Apaches once."

"I'll gladly take you up on your generous offer, kind sir." Mary playfully did a curtsy.

Now Fargo did reach out. He kissed her hard, passion boiling in him like water in a pot. If it weren't for her kids and Rika, he would have taken her right then and there, snow or no snow, cold or no cold.

"Mmm. That was nice. I don't have a lot of experience but you're the best kisser who ever lived."

"If I didn't know better, I'd swear you were drunk."

Fargo kept on scanning the forest as they talked. Either it was his imagination, or something had moved off in the trees. "You should get some rest. We'll stay here half an hour, then push on."

"Is it safe?"

Fargo nodded at Nelly and Jayce. "Safe has nothing to do with it. They won't last a mile if they don't get some sleep."

"Very well."

Mary picked another tree and sat on a patch of dry pine needles. She leaned her shoulder against the bole and closed her eyes.

Weariness nipped at Fargo but he shook it off. He paced, then hunkered where he could watch the Harpers and the forest both. Snow fell from a limb with a muffled thud. A sparrow chirped. Otherwise, the woods were quiet.

Perhaps too quiet.

Fargo's eyelids became heavy and he started to doze. With an oath, he roused his sluggish senses. It would be all Rika needed: him to fall asleep and be as easy to take as a newborn babe.

A feeling came over him, a conviction that he was being watched. Rika, waiting for his chance.

Fargo glanced at the horses and then out over the flatland and then to his left into the woods—and saw an Indian so close he could hit him with a snowball. Fargo blinked, and the Indian was gone. Straightening, he placed his hand on the Colt. He wondered if he'd really seen him or only thought he did. Warily, he moved toward the spot.

The woods were deathly still; even the sparrow had gone quiet.

Tracks didn't lie, and there in the snow were moccasin prints.

Sometimes Fargo could tell from the shape and the stitching which tribe fashioned any given footwear. But that was when the prints were in mud or soft earth or it was so dusty every detail showed. Here in the snow there wasn't much to go on.

Fargo debated giving chase and decided against it. It would be foolhardy, bordering on stupid, to leave Mary and the kids alone. He backed away. Why invite an arrow between the shoulder blades?

Now he had a possible hostile as well as a killer to deal with. One good thing: Seeing the warrior had jarred him awake.

He let about half an hour go by, then shook Mary's shoulder and had her wake her kids. Nelly and Jayce were snails. They sat up slowly and stood slowly and climbed on the sorrel slower than molasses.

Fargo was impatient. For all he knew, Cud Sten and the rest of the outlaws were after them, too. The more miles they put behind them, the safer they would be. From Sten, anyway.

Mary smiled and fluffed her hair as she brought the dun up next to the Ovaro. "Thank you for letting us sleep. I feel rested. I take it there's been no sign of that man you think is following us?"

"Not yet."

"Maybe he isn't back there. Maybe he never came after us and you're fretting over nothing."

"And maybe buffalo will sprout wings and fly. Don't make the mistake of assuming anything."

"Do you ever make mistakes? I only ask because I've never met anyone so sure of himself as you are. You always seem to know just what to do."

"Fat lot of good it's done me, lady. I've lost count of my blunders."

"It's Mary, remember? After what we did, I should think you could at least call me by my name."

Fargo sighed. It was just like a woman to think that since she had shared her body, she was entitled to some sort of claim on the man she had shared her body with.

"I heard that." Mary sounded hurt.

"Heard what, Ma?" Nelly and Jayce had come up on the other side. Where before Nelly had been handling the reins and Jayce had ridden behind her, now he was in the saddle and she had her arms around him.

"A jay," Mary said. "I thought I heard a jay."

The sun climbed higher. The temperature warmed but not enough to melt the white mantle.

Fargo checked behind them so many times he lost count. Not once did he spot a hostile or Rika. But one or both were back there. He amused himself by imagining the result should Rika and the warrior stumble on each other.

Sunset splashed pink and yellow across the western sky. Amid lengthening shadows, Fargo rode along the tree line seeking a spot to stop for the night. Mary could scarcely keep her head up and the kids were near the point of exhaustion.

He came on a gully rimmed by trees that had sheltered it from the worst of the snow. The sides weren't too steep and the bottom was wide enough and flat enough to make for a comfortable camp. Dismounting, he walked the Ovaro down, and in turn did the same with each of the other mounts. Next he gathered firewood, which took a lot longer than it ordinarily would. Most of the downed limbs were covered with snow and too wet to burn. He persevered, though, until he needed both arms to carry it all.

By then the sun was almost gone. Twilight was about to fall, and after that, the Stygian mantle of night.

Nelly and Jayce were asleep. They were bundled to their chins, as serene as cherubs.

Mary was huddled beside them, shivering, a blanket over her shoulders. "There you are! I was getting worried."

"Hear or see anything?"

"It's been as peaceful as a church service. I've dozed off once or twice." Mary smiled. "I was hoping you'd make it back before I passed out."

Fargo broke some of the branches for firewood. The rest he stacked to use later. He added a handful of dry grass he had found, then took out his fire steel and flint. It took five tries before a spark caught, and he fanned a tiny flame to life. Wisps of smoke rose, growing thicker as the branches ignited. Soon the welcoming crackle of flames warmed his fingers and face.

Mary came over and held her hands to the fire. "Mercy me, that feels good. I'm so cold, you could set me on fire and I'd take a week to burn."

In short order Fargo had strips of cow meat roasting on the end of sticks. The aroma set his mouth to watering.

Jayce woke up and commenced to sniffing and looking about. When he saw the meat, he scrambled out from under his blanket and crawled over on his hands and knees. "I could eat that raw."

Soon Nelly was up. She joined them in hovering over the sizzling morsels, her anticipation so keen she appeared to be in pain.

The moment Fargo announced the meat was done, they grabbed sticks and tore into it with zeal that wolves would envy.

Fargo had to admit it was delicious. He chewed slowly, savoring.

With every swallow a little more vitality flowed through his veins. It would be best to ration the meat, but he roasted another piece for each one of them. It still wasn't enough. When he was done, he was still hungry.

Jayce licked his fingers and thumbs, smacking his lips between licks.

"What do you say?" Mary asked him.

"It was good."

"That's not what I meant. When someone treats you to a meal, you're supposed to say 'Thank you.'"

"Thanks, Ma."

"Not me, silly. Thank Mr. Fargo. He cooked it."

"He sure is a good friend, isn't he, Ma?"

"He sure is."

Whether because of that, or on her own account, later, when it came time for the children to turn in, Nelly gave Fargo a hug. "Thank you for being so nice to us. It's been so long, I'd almost forgotten what nice was."

Since his sister had come over, Jayce did, too. But he just stood there, rocking on his heels, unsure of what to do until Fargo held out a hand for him to shake.

Mary shooed them under their blankets. She tucked them in and said prayers with them and then pecked each on the forehead and advised them to get a good night's rest. Strolling to the fire, she sat closer to him than before. "You're a good influence on them."

Fargo tried to recollect the last time anyone had said that about him; he couldn't. "They should sleep the whole night through."

"Yes. As tired as they were. And then the meat. I imagine it would take a lot of noise to wake them."

Fargo broke a limb and added half to the fire. He didn't attach any special meaning to her remark.

"Yes, sir," Mary said, and shifted so she was closer. "It's going to be a long night."

"You'll sleep as good as they do," Fargo predicted.

"I suppose I will, provided I can relax. All day I've been tense with dread." Mary shifted again.

"I'll keep watch." Fargo didn't ask her to help although he knew very well he wouldn't be able to stay awake much past midnight. He was worn-out. He needed rest as much as they did.

"Is that necessary? We haven't had any trouble all day. Why not catch up on your sleep, too?"

"I'll get what I can."

"What you need," Mary said, "is to take your mind off all

that's happened. You need to forget about Cud Sten and Rika and the rest." She moved so that when he poked at the fire, he couldn't raise his arm without brushing against her.

Only then did Fargo catch on. He looked at her and said the first thought that popped into his head: "Oh, hell."

"What?"

"Are you drunk?"

"I should say not."

"Crazy, then? We're being hunted. There are Indians about. It has to be twenty above, if that. By two in the morning it will be five below."

"So?"

"So you really want it that much?"

"I do."

Skye Fargo shook his head. "Women."

17

Mary Harper pressed against Fargo and gave him a look he had seen a thousand times. A look that said she was a ripe cherry waiting to be tasted and all he had to do was reach up and pluck the cherry from the tree.

"What about women?" she teased.

"Now?"

Mary laughed, caught herself, and glanced at her children. "I better keep the noise down."

Fargo could feel the warmth of her body against his. He admired the suggestive sweep of enticing thighs and remembered her passion, and he twitched below his belt.

Mary clasped his hand in both of hers and rubbed it. "You have big, strong hands. I like that in a man."

"You gush nice. I like that in a woman."

Mary blinked and started to laugh again. Covering her mouth, she giggled and said, "Oh, my. You come right out with it, don't you?"

"No, you do."

"I do what?"

"Come right out with it."

Mary managed to smother her mirth enough not to wake Nelly or Jayce. "Thanks. You've drained the tension right from me."

"Then I guess there's no need for the other," Fargo said. But the notion of having her again was making him stiff where it would do both of them the most good.

"I never said that. Don't you want me?"

Fargo cupped her twin mounds and squeezed, hard. "What do you think?"

Mary threw back her head and gasped. She gripped his wrists and pulled his hands tighter against her. The tip of her tongue rimmed her lips, and when she looked at him, her eyes were pools of raw lust. "Yes, I like that. I like that a whole lot."

So did Fargo. He massaged and kneaded. Her nipples became tacks, poking into his palms. He pinched one and then the other, and Mary squirmed in delight.

"I've wanted you so much. The other night, you did something to me."

Fargo hoped she wasn't confusing passion with something else. He shut her up by covering her mouth in a long kiss. Her tongue met his in wet need. The warmth of her body and the warmth of the fire combined to make him hot with desire.

"Mmm," Mary husked when they parted for breath. "I've said it before, I'll say it again. You're the best kisser ever."

"Says the woman who's only been with one other man." Fargo smiled to lessen the sting in case she took it the wrong way.

"Go ahead. Rub it in. But I've always been a one-man woman, and Frank was my man until he died. When I get back to civilization, I'll be on the lookout for another. Until then . . ." Mary grinned and fused her lips to his.

The sigh of the wind, the blowing snow, the howl of a wolf, and the cries of coyotes—Fargo was aware of it all. A part of his mind stayed focused on the world around them, probing for the slightest hint of danger.

Mary, meanwhile, explored him with her hands, running them over his shoulders and down the shirt she had lent him and then under and up over his washboard muscles. "I like your body," she whispered in his ear.

Fargo liked hers. He ran a hand through her hair, and with his other, he gripped her bottom. He pulled her to him so they were bosom to chest and leg to leg.

"Goodness," Mary breathed, and reaching between his legs, she began fondling him.

A branch popped in the fire.

High on the mountain a cougar screamed.

Fargo glanced at the horses. All three stood with their heads bowed, weary from the long hours of hard travel. None had their ears pricked or showed the least alarm. It was safe to give free rein to his craving.

Fargo pulled Mary onto his lap and she parted her legs wide to grant him access. But he wasn't about to plunge right in. He kissed and licked her throat. He nipped an earlobe. He slid a hand under her dress and caressed her leg.

"Lordy," Mary gasped.

Fargo rubbed in small circles until he reached her knee. He traced a finger along her inner thigh and she quivered.

"Please," she said.

"When I'm ready."

She had started this; he would finish it.

Mary cupped his chin and tried to suck his mouth into hers. Her yearning was at a fever pitch. Loosening his belt, she swooped her hand low and held him where it would drive any man to the heights of delight. "Do you like that?"

"What do you think?" Fargo retorted in a voice that didn't sound anything like his.

"I think your stallion should be jealous."

"I think you talk too much."

For long, languid minutes they kissed and groped and fondled. Fargo's manhood was iron. Mary's thighs were almost as hot as the fire. She was even hotter higher up—hot and wet, for when he lightly ran a finger along her slit, his finger grew moist with her dew.

"Ohh, more of that, if you please."

Fargo obliged. Each flick of her tiny knob brought a convulsion of release. She ground against his hand, her hips bucking. Her groans and mews filled the air, but never too loud. Hers was a cautious abandon.

Fargo was cautious, too. He glanced at her kids, making sure they were still asleep, and then at the horses. The Ovaro had its head up but showed no sign of being agitated.

"What's wrong?"

Fargo realized he had stopped stroking her. "Nothing," he said throatily, and took up where he had left off. A hard lance of his finger, and he was in her velvety sheath up to the knuckle. She came up off his lap, then sank down with a soft moan.

"The woman you take for a wife will be the luckiest woman alive," Mary whispered, and commenced to thrust her hips in rhythm with the thrust of his finger.

Fargo added a second finger and her inner walls rippled. Her hips churned. She was wetter than ever.

The Ovaro was staring into the gloom. Something had caught its interest, but it didn't nicker or stamp.

Fargo glanced in the same direction but all he saw were the white humps of trees. If Rika or the warrior were out there, now was when they would strike. He kept on pumping his hand, but he didn't take his eyes off the woods until the Ovaro lowered its head again.

Mary's fingers enclosed his pole.

Fargo wasn't expecting it, and it took his breath away. He rose high enough to drop his pants to his knees, then hiked her dress and lightly touched the tip of his member to her slit.

"Now. Please, now."

"Now," Fargo said, and rammed up into her. For all of five seconds, she was rigid with a flood of emotion, and then her body came alive. She met each of his thrusts with abandon.

Faster and faster they rose toward the summit. Harder and harder they sought to trigger mutual release.

Suddenly Mary gushed, her mouth wide but no sounds coming out. The whites of her eyes showed, and her eyelids fluttered.

The very next thrust sent Fargo over the brink. It was the end of him and the beginning of him all over again. It was the moment he lived for. There was nothing else like it.

They coasted to a stop, and sagged, Mary's cheek on his chest and her eyes closed in grateful weariness.

"You're marvelous. Truly marvelous."

"Don't tell the Ovaro."

His remark brought a snort and a light laugh. "I'll miss you when we go our own ways. You've brought me out of myself. You've reminded me of what it's like to be alive."

"You've reminded me of why I like women, so we're even." Fargo tugged his pants on; the air was cold on his private parts. Once he was buckled, he pulled her dress down over her legs to keep her warm.

"Thank you, kind sir. I hope you don't mind me throwing myself at you like that."

Women, Fargo reflected, said the silliest things.

Mary closed her eyes and forked an arm around his neck. "I could go to sleep right here in your lap."

"Better turn in, then." Fargo helped her stand and walked with her to her blanket. She kissed him on the cheek, tenderly touched the spot she had kissed, and sank down.

Fargo returned to the fire. He added another branch. The wolves and the coyotes had gone quiet and the near-total silence made every slight sound he made seem twice as loud. He scanned the trees and checked the horses, and convinced it was safe, he threw a blanket over his shoulders and huddled close to the fire for the warmth.

Time crawled on claws of ice.

Fargo didn't know how long he could stay awake, but the

longer he could, the safer they'd be. He struggled. His body was close to shutting down, he was so tired. He kept forgetting that he hadn't fully recovered from his clash with the wolves.

Eventually the inevitable happened. Fargo's eyes refused to stay open and his brain refused to stay alert. He drifted in and out, snapping awake now and then to stare numbly at the fire and add more fuel. Then he would go under again, dreaming chaotic dreams.

The last time he fell asleep, he slept the longest. He came back to wakefulness slowly, sensing that it had been hours and that it must be close to dawn. He yawned and went to stretch and opened his eyes, and froze with his arms half in the air.

"Morning," Rika said.

Fargo was awake in a heartbeat. His gut churned but outwardly he stayed calm. "What time is it?"

"The sun will rise soon." Rika was in a squat on the other side of the fire, the Henry trained on Fargo's chest, the hammer already thumbed back.

"I knew I should have tried harder to stay awake."

"I did my sleeping while you were making your camp and eating. About midnight I got up, and I've been waiting my chance ever since."

"I'm surprised I'm still alive."

Rika frowned. "It's not up to me or you wouldn't be. Cud wants you breathing."

"He wants to do it himself," Fargo guessed.

"I've never seen him so worked up about killing someone," Rika revealed. "You killed Tull and you killed Boyce. No one kills his men and lives. He'll have you staked out and then beat you to death, breaking a bone at a time, unless you beg him to end it."

"I wouldn't count on the begging."

"You might be the toughest son of a bitch alive, but you'll

beg. I've seen him do it too many times. Some men can take having their arms and their legs broken. Some can take their fingers being snapped, or their ribs staved in. But when he uses that club of his on their crotch, they break." Rika grinned. "You'll beg, all right."

"And them?" Fargo asked with a nod at the Harpers.

"Cud might spare them. He's fond of the woman. He'd like to kill her brats but it would upset her too much."

"A fine gent, Cud Sten," Fargo said sarcastically.

A rare smile curled Rika's mouth. "Cud Sten is the most vicious bastard who ever lived. He killed his own mother when he was fifteen and he's been killing ever since. Or maybe killing is the wrong word. Cud *destroys* people. He tortures them and then he laughs in their faces and finishes them off. He enjoys it. He loves to break bones. He loves to hear people scream and cry and beg. He loves it more than he loves anything."

It was the most Fargo ever heard Rika say, and he noticed the excitement that crept into Rika's own voice. "You love it, too."

"Almost as much as Cud does. It's why him and me have been together so long. We both like to kill." Rika chuckled. "They say friends should have something in common."

"You could let *them* go on," Fargo said with another nod at the Harpers. "I'm the one Cud wants."

"And tell Cud what? That they got away from me? Do you honestly think he'd believe it?" Rika gazed at their sleeping forms. "They mean nothing to me. Whether they live or they die, it's all the same. Hell, I'd kill them myself if Cud wanted me to."

The whole time they talked, Fargo had been inching his hand toward his Colt. The blanket over his shoulders hid the movement. Another few inches and he would take his chances rather than let himself be taken back to face Cud Sten's club.

"We'll wait until sunrise and then wake them," Rika was saying. "I suppose you'd better feed them, too, or the brats will whine all the way back."

Fargo's fingers were so close to the Colt, all it would take was a flick of his wrist and Cud Sten would be even madder.

But suddenly, unexpectedly, Rika snapped the Henry to his shoulder. "Ever been shot?"

"A few times."

"Want to add another time?"

"Not particularly, no."

"That's too bad. A man as dumb as you has to expect to be shot once in a while." Rika took deliberate aim.

18

Skye Fargo imitated one of the snowbound trees except to say, "I thought you were taking me back alive."

"Just so you're breathing." Rika wagged the Henry. "Right now I want you to shed that six-shooter you've been reaching for. Get rid of the blanket first."

Fargo looked into the muzzle of his own rifle and did as he was told.

He started to move the blanket aside. That was when he saw Jayce Harper. The boy had woken up and was on his feet.

Rika had his back to the Harpers and hadn't noticed. "That's it. Play it smart and do it slow."

Jayce looked at Fargo and put a finger to his lips. Then he bent and silently scooped up some snow.

Fargo almost shouted not to try anything—it would only get him killed. But something stayed the impulse. Every nerve tingling, he saw Jayce straighten and mold the snow until it was hard and round. "The law will catch up to Sten sooner or later. You know that, don't you?"

"The six-shooter," Rika said.

Jayce snuck toward Rika, placing each foot carefully.

Fargo's fate hung on the boy succeeding. To distract Rika he said, "You should strike off on your own."

Rika's brow furrowed. "I just told you that him and me are pards."

Jayce was only five feet away.

"You said it yourself," Fargo said. "He's as vicious as they come. One day you'll do or say something he doesn't like and he'll turn on you."

"You're up to something."

Jayce stopped and looked at Fargo and then at the back of Rika's head. He cocked his arm to throw.

Fargo had to do it just right. He couldn't raise his voice or give Rika any cause to think he was in danger. As calmly as he could, he remarked, "It looks like one of the Harpers is up."

Rika turned his head, just his head, exactly as Fargo wanted, and the instant he did, Jayce threw the snowball at his face. The boy threw hard and true, and Rika jumped up and took a step back in surprise, swiping a hand at his eyes to clear them.

That was all the opening Fargo needed. He swept his Colt up and out, intending to shoot Rika where he stood, but the Colt's hammer snagged on the blanket. He twisted to free it but it wouldn't come free. And then Rika, blinking snow away, was turning toward him and bringing the Henry to bear, and Fargo did the only thing he could think of to do: He dived across the fire. Sun-hot heat seared his chest, and then his shoulder slammed into Rika's legs and he wrapped his other arm around Rika's ankles and they crashed to the snow.

The Henry blasted but the shot must have missed because Fargo didn't feel any pain. He rolled, and nearly had his face caved in by a sweep of the Henry's stock. Lunging, he grabbed the barrel.

Rika kicked, knocking Fargo backward. He tried to lever another round into the chamber as he rose to his knees.

Fargo sprang. This time his shoulder caught Rika across the chest and down they went. Rika let go of the Henry. His hand disappeared up a sleeve, and when it reappeared it held a knife. He stabbed up and in. It was only by a hair that the blade missed and snagged in the blanket as the Colt had done.

Fargo kneed Rika in the groin. For most men, that would have been enough but all Rika did was scowl and jerk on his knife while simultaneously dipping a hand to the holster on his hip.

Fargo still had hold of his Colt, and it was still caught in the blanket but a blanket wouldn't stop a bullet. He jammed the muzzle against Rika's ribs and stroked the trigger. Rika jumped, his teeth bared in a grimace. Again he sought to bury his blade. Fargo had the hammer back and he fired a third time and a fourth.

Rika lay gasping and bubbling crimson. "Damn you. You shot me to pieces."

Fargo stood. He kicked the knife from Rika's grasp and Jayce picked it up. Fargo pointed the Colt at Rika's face, then caught sight of Mary with her arm around Nelly.

"Do it," Rika said.

Fargo lowered his arm.

"Bastard." Rika coughed and out came more blood. "I should have shot you at the cabin or before."

"You should have," Fargo agreed.

Rika's eyes moved in circles, then steadied. "Killed by a blanket and a damn snot with a snowball."

"We never know, do we?"

Rika swallowed. "It won't do you any good. Cud will kill you yet. Finding you in this snow will be easy."

"I hope they come." Fargo disliked to leave a lead affray unfinished. Otherwise, he would be looking over his shoulder the rest of his days.

"I hope you rot in hell," Rika said, and died.

Mary came over, Nelly clinging to her, and put her hand on Jayce's shoulder. "I saw what you did, son. That was very brave."

"I didn't want him to hurt Mr. Fargo."

"I'm obliged—Jayce." Fargo almost said "boy." He threw off the blanket that had caused so much trouble and began reloading.

Mary let go of Nelly. "I heard what he told you. How soon before Cud is after us?"

"No way of telling." Sten didn't impress Fargo as being the most patient man alive.

"What do we do?"

"We eat breakfast," Fargo said. They could stay in the saddle longer on full stomachs. Skip the noon stop, and push on until nightfall.

"We have time?"

Fargo nudged the body. "We do now." He went through Rika's clothes. He gave the wrist sheath and the knife to Jayce. He passed a handful of coins to Mary, who shook her head and said she couldn't accept them.

"Why not?"

"Who knows how he came by them? It could be blood money. I wouldn't want to touch it, let alone keep it."

"You kept Tull's."

"This is different."

Fargo didn't see how. But he pocketed the coins himself.

"We should start to dig," Mary proposed. "It will take us half the day, the ground as hard as it is."

"No."

"We can't leave the body lying there. It wouldn't be right."

"Would you rather have Sten catch up?" Fargo bent, slid a hand under each of Rika's arms, and dragged him toward the trees. Jayce leaped to help by taking hold of one foot. To Fargo's surprise, Nelly took the other. It was slow going; the snow impeded every step.

Mary followed. "Tell me true, Skye. What are our odds of reaching a settlement or a fort before Cud catches up to us."

"It depends on whether Cud is waiting at your cabin or whether he sent Rika on ahead and then came after him."

"Lordy." Mary gazed back the way they came. "Then Cud might be dogging our scent right this minute. What do we do?"

"We eat," Fargo reiterated. But first they dragged the body twenty-five yards, and Fargo rolled it behind a log and covered it with snow.

As they walked back, Mary cleared her throat. "May I ask you something?"

Fargo hoped it wouldn't have anything to do with him and her. "So long as your vocal cords work."

"What? Oh." Mary grinned halfheartedly. "No, the question is this." She put one hand on Nelly and another on Jayce. "Are we slowing you down?"

"What kind of question is that?"

"We are, aren't we? I bet if you were on your own, you could get away. But with us you have to go slower than you would. Because of us, Sten might catch you and kill you."

Fargo shrugged.

"I thought so. The last thing I want is for you to die because of me. I'm sure my children agree. So I have a proposal for you." Mary grinned self-consciously. "Not *that* kind of proposal. I want you to go on ahead and forget about us."

"Any other dumb ideas?"

"Please. Save yourself while you can. We'll be all right. Cud will come along and take us back."

"He might shoot you, as mad as he'll be." Fargo shook his head. "We stick together. When I ride on, so do you. If you refuse to keep going, so do I."

"Why must men be so pigheaded? I'm trying to save your life."

"It's *my* life."

"We don't mind if you leave us," Nelly said. "Really we don't." But her fear put the lie to her claim.

Jayce was the only honest one. "I will. We'll die without him."

"Enough of that kind of talk," Mary said.

"I'm only saying what you did, Ma."

That quieted her. They came to the fire, and Fargo went to his saddlebags and fished out his coffeepot and coffee. He liked a steaming cup every morning, and he wasn't going to deny himself one of his few creature comforts because of Cud Sten. For water he melted snow.

Mary had brought along what was left of the flour and sugar and a few other things, and she set to work making flapjacks.

Jayce and Nelly watched her like those starving wolves had eyed Fargo.

Before long Mary was humming as she worked. The kids talked and joked and smiled.

Fargo sipped coffee and pretended to listen. He was scouring the woods. He'd caught a hint of movement, brown against the white. It could be a deer. It could be an elk. Or it could be a warrior in buckskins.

They didn't have plates or silverware, so they placed the flapjacks on their legs and ate with their fingers.

Fargo was famished. He could have eaten a dozen. Then the dun nickered for no reason that he could see. It made him realize he had overlooked something. "Damn," he blurted.

Mary, about to take a bite, looked over in concern. "Is something wrong?"

"I'm getting sloppy." Fargo finished and stood and went over and held out the Henry.

"What's this for?"

"Protection. I shouldn't be gone long."

"Gone?" Mary repeated, and she and the children rose and clustered close. "You're leaving us alone?"

142

"Fifteen minutes ago you wanted me to ride off for good." Fargo placed the rifle in her hands. "If you need me, fire a shot and I'll come as fast as I can."

"But why must you go?"

"Rika's horse."

The footprints were plain enough. Fargo backtracked into the trees. They led him to a spruce Rika had hunkered under to spy on them. From the spruce the trail led a meandering course from tree to tree and bush to bush. Rika had used every available bit of cover to get close to them.

Abruptly, the tracks made a beeline that brought Fargo to a clearing. And there, tied to a tree on the other side, was the claybank. It snorted but didn't shy when Fargo gripped the bridle. He stroked it and spoke quietly, then undid the reins and started back.

Fargo took three steps, and stopped.

Imprinted in the snow a few feet away were other tracks. Someone—several someones—had come out of the forest and stood awhile, then gone back into the forest without taking the claybank with them. Those someones, Fargo suspected, were Indians.

He climbed on the claybank. He had enough problems without hostiles. But *were* they hostile, given they hadn't taken the horse? He gigged the claybank, heading straight for the Harpers, worried that maybe the warriors had paid them a visit in his absence. But they were anxiously waiting, the children by the fire, Mary pacing with the Henry.

Fargo allowed himself another cup of coffee, and then they were under way. He rode the Ovaro. Mary had the dun, Jayce rode the sorrel, and Nelly was on the claybank. For over a mile they had easy going. Then the flatland changed to country broken by ravines and plateaus.

Fargo picked the easiest route. Sometimes that meant swinging wide to avoid a treacherous slope or a ravine too steep for the horses to safely descend. It slowed them terribly, until he chafed at the delays. But there was no help for it.

A clear slope rose. Or so it appeared. Fargo wondered, though, if under the snow there might be loose rocks and earth that could break away and bring a horse down.

"Mr. Fargo?" Jayce said.

"Just a minute." Fargo was studying the slope. He would go first, and if he made it to the top, the others could follow in his hoofprints.

"Mr. Fargo?" Jayce said again.

"I said just a minute."

"But it's important."

Fargo shifted in the saddle. "What is?"

Jayce shifted in the saddle, too, and pointed back the way they had come. "Them," he said.

Nelly gasped.

"No!" Mary exclaimed.

"Yes," Fargo said.

Five riders were a half mile off.

It was Cud Sten and his killers.

19

Fargo reined to the right and shouted for the Harpers to follow him. Their one hope was to get over the ridge before Sten arrived. He searched for a way to reach the top that wouldn't result in disaster. Ahead, the slope ended at a belt of forest. He could find a spot for the Harpers to hide, and then end this thing once and for all. He was tired of running. It went against his grain.

Mary was grim. Nelly showed terror. Jayce was intent on keeping up with the rest of them.

Sten and his men had brought their mounts to a gallop. Even at that distance Fargo recognized the red-haired Lear and the short man called Howell. He'd never learned the names of the other two.

The snow became deeper. Fargo hadn't counted on that, but he should have; snow nearly always fell heavier at higher elevations. He goaded the Ovaro on, breaking the snow for the others. The night's rest had lent the stallion new vitality, and it showed no signs of tiring.

The air was colder. It cut into Fargo's lungs like icy knives. But that was good. The cold would keep them alert.

It seemed to take forever but it wasn't more than five minutes before they reached the woodland. Fargo drew rein and the others came up on either side of him.

Sten and company were less than a quarter of a mile away and had spread out.

"What will we do?" Nelly asked.

"What we've been doing."

"They'll catch us. And he'll do terrible things to Ma. And maybe beat Jayce and me."

"Over my dead body," Mary vowed.

Fargo entered the trees but only went far enough to keep from being seen from below. Dismounting, he shucked the Henry from the saddle scabbard and gave it to Mary after she climbed down.

"I thought you'd want to use it," she said.

"I need range." Fargo went to the sorrel and yanked the Sharps from the scabbard. A cartridge was already in the chamber. He told them to stay put and walked back to within a few steps of the open slope and squatted behind a tree.

Sten and company were coming on hard.

Fargo gauged the distance. He adjusted the sight and tucked the Sharps to his shoulder. He aimed at Cud Sten. Sten was the key. Kill him and the others might give it up.

Fargo thumbed back the hammer. He pulled on the rear trigger to set the front trigger, then curled his finger around the front trigger. He held his breath to steady the shot, and when he was absolutely and positively sure, he stroked the front trigger. Thunder echoed off the peaks.

Hundreds of yards out, Cud Sten's horse stumbled. Not because it was hit. It stumbled a split instant *before* Fargo fired, and the slug that was to core Sten's chest missed. Cud promptly drew rein and bellowed at his men.

Swearing, Fargo reloaded. If he was superstitious, he might be inclined to think Cud Sten lived a charmed life.

Sten and his men had swung down and were on the other side of their mounts, using their horses as shields. Rifles cracked and lead thwacked nearby trees. They had a fair idea of where he was.

"Stay down, children."

Fargo turned. Mary and the kids were huddled only a few yards away. "Don't you ever listen?"

146

"We were worried."

Fargo swore again, in his head. He nodded toward the figures out on the snow. "I'll keep them pinned down as long as I can. I want you to take your horses and go. I'll catch up when I can."

"No."

"Damn it, woman."

"We're not you. We don't ride all that well. We're bound to take a spill and maybe break a leg or an arm. Or get lost."

"I'll find you," Fargo insisted.

"Maybe too late. No. We're staying and that's final."

They begged him with their faces.

Fargo made up his mind then and there to never again get involved with a woman with kids. Not that he would stick to it. When it came to good-looking women, he'd never met a pair of thighs he didn't want to spread.

"You'll let us stay, then?" Mary asked when he didn't say anything.

Fargo just looked at her.

Out on the snow the firing had stopped and Sten and his men were peering over their saddles.

"Mount up," Fargo said. "I'll be there in a minute." They left, and he raised the Sharps and took deliberate aim at the horse Cud Sten was behind. He didn't want to do it. He didn't want to shoot a horse. But he had to. The horse would drop and he'd have a clear shot at Sten. He thumbed back the hammer and set the trigger and was ready.

Nelly Harper screamed.

Fargo jerked around. Mary yelled something and the horses commenced to whinny, and he was up and running, kicking snow every which way. He thought maybe it was Indians, but he burst through the trees and dug in his heels in consternation at the sight of the Harpers trying to hold on to the reins of their mounts. Mary had hold of both the dun and the Ovaro, and the dun was trying to rear and kick.

147

It had cause. Crouched nearby was a large mountain lion about to spring. Fangs bared, tail twitching, it uttered a ferocious snarl.

Jayce was nearly pulled off his feet by the sorrel, which wheeled to bolt. Fargo got there in a few bounds, seized the reins, and brought it to a stop. Then he was past them and charging toward the mountain lion, raising the rifle as he ran.

The mountain lion saw him. Cats were unpredictable and this one was no exception. It wanted fresh meat, but the shouts and the whinnies and the commotion were too much for it. One moment it was there, poised to rip and rend, the next it was a tawny streak, lost amid the trees.

Fargo lowered the Sharps and did more swearing. By now Sten and his men were racing for the trees. He had to get the Harpers out. "Mount up!" he roared. He had to help Nelly because the claybank wouldn't stop prancing.

Fargo shoved the Sharps into the sorrel's saddle scabbard, then ran to the Ovaro. Mary was on the dun and held the stallion's reins, and the Henry, out to him. Forking leather, he looked but couldn't see Sten and his men.

"Ride for your lives." Fargo led off.

Mary dropped back so she was behind Nelly and Jayce and could help them if either flagged.

Fargo couldn't waste precious seconds trying to pick the easiest way. He just rode, avoiding obstacles, and there were a god-awful lot of them: snow-covered trees, huge drifts, logs and boulders next to impossible to spot until he was almost on top of them. He was constantly reining this way and that.

The Harpers kept up. Sweat slicked their faces and they were as pale as the snow, but they rode as they had never ridden in their lives.

Fargo felt strangely proud of them. Strange because they weren't his wife and kids. Pride suggested he cared more than he did.

From somewhere to their rear rose shouts.

The forest went on and on, unending white chaos. The strain on Fargo's eyes, the relentless glare, and the strain on his nerves from the endless near brushes with disaster began to tell. He could only imagine how hard it was for the Harpers, who weren't used to much riding, and none whatsoever like this.

Fargo kept hoping the forest would end. On an open plain, they could widen their lead. When, at long last, the trees began to thin, he smiled and went to shout to the Harpers. But the shout died in his throat. The forest *did* end—near the edge of a precipice.

Hauling on the reins, Fargo brought the Ovaro to a sliding stop with barely three feet to spare. Twisting, he motioned and bellowed, "Stop! Stop!"

Nelly reined up sharply. So did Mary. But either Jayce didn't hear the warning or he was too slow to react, because the sorrel went flying toward the brink at a headlong gallop.

Mary screamed.

Fargo darted out a hand as the boy went by. He seized Jayce's arm and held on, virtually tearing Jayce from the saddle. The sorrel didn't stop or slow but went on over. A strident whinny pierced the air. Fargo dropped Jayce in the snow, vaulted down, and ran to the edge. He saw the sorrel, tumbling end over end, hit among boulders. The effect was as if a keg of black powder went off. The snow exploded. So did parts of the horse. What was left of it lay kicking and squealing, its insides oozing from its ruptured belly, shattered bones sticking from its hide.

Mary had alighted and was holding Jayce to her. Nelly, still on the claybank, gazed sadly down.

"Get off," Fargo directed. He snatched the Ovaro's reins and made for an isolated circle of trees that grew close by. "Follow me!" He figured he had two minutes, maybe three. "Hurry!"

Fargo was in for it now. He had to make his stand with

his back to a cliff. And he only had one rifle; the Sharps had gone over with the sorrel.

The trees were lodgepole pines. Arrayed in tightly spaced ranks, they offered some protection. Fargo got the Ovaro in among them and yanked the Henry out. Nelly came next, tugging on the claybank's reins. Mary was leading the dun and had put Jayce in the saddle.

"I'd like to thank you for saving his life."

"Later," Fargo said.

The outlaws had caught up. Shadowy figures were moving about in the forest. But they wisely didn't show themselves.

"We're trapped, aren't we?" Mary asked.

Fargo didn't reply. There was no need.

Mary walked on but she was back in a minute, hunkered beside him. "I tied the horses and told Nelly and Jayce to stay with them." She showed him her hand, and what was in it. "Nelly found these in Rika's saddlebags."

It was a pistol made by the Volcanic Repeating Arms Company. Only .31 caliber, it wasn't much of a man stopper, but it was better than nothing. She also had a box of cartridges.

"Do you know how to load it?"

Mary sat and placed the ammunition in her lap. She fiddled with the lever—the pistol was a lever-action model—and said, "No."

Fargo showed her. The Volcanic held ten shots. Between that and his Henry and the Colt and the Remington, they had considerable lead to spare, should Cud Sten take it into his head to rush them. "Here." He gave it back to her.

Mary hefted the pistol and frowned. "I doubt I'll hit much of anything. I've only ever shot a revolver twice my whole life."

Fargo turned to the forest. During the brief time he had been distracted, the outlaws had gone to ground. He had no idea where they were. Then a head popped up from behind a mound of snow. Lear, it looked like. The head promptly ducked down again.

"What will they do?" Mary asked. "Wait until dark and close in?"

"It depends on how badly Cud Sten wants us dead."

As if Sten had somehow heard, the forest erupted with shots. Slugs whistled and sizzled, smacking the lodgepoles, shattering limbs.

"Nelly and Jayce!" Mary cried, and started to rise.

Flattening, Fargo pulled her down beside him. She resisted, but only until he said, "They're far enough back. They should be safe."

Twenty to thirty shots were fired, and then silence.

"Shouldn't we shoot back?" Mary whispered.

"Not until we have something to shoot at."

"Ma?" Nelly hollered, and was echoed by her brother.

"I'm all right, honey," Mary answered. "Stay where you are and do as I told you." She said quietly to Fargo, "If you and I are shot, they're to make a run for it."

Fargo could predict the outcome. The kids wouldn't get far. Hunger or the cold would finish them.

Mary placed her hand on his. "Will you think less of me if I admit I'm scared?"

"Only a jackass wouldn't be."

That was when Cud Sten shouted, "Hey, Mary gal! Have you missed me?"

"Go to hell!" Mary replied, and bit her lower lip. "Darn me. My kids heard that. And me always on them about behaving like a gentleman and a lady."

It bewildered Fargo, her concern over her language at a time like this.

"Why, Mary, I do believe you are cross with me. Yet you're the one who ran out on me. I should be cross at you."

Mary's mouth was a slit.

"How about you, simpleton?" Cud called out. "Have you missed me, too?"

Fargo knew what Sten was doing: finding out if either of them had been hit. He kept his mouth shut.

"Mary gal! Why doesn't your friend answer? Could it be he can't? Did he stake a slug, gal? Is that it?"

Mary opened her mouth to respond, but Fargo put a finger to his lips and shook his head.

"Come on, gal. You can tell me."

Mary was a volcano ready to erupt.

"Well, now," Cud said, brimming with confidence. "Seems to me I can end this sooner than I reckoned. Tell you what, gal. You and your sprouts come out with your hands in the air, and I give you my solemn word none of you will be harmed."

Mary looked at Fargo, and he shook his head.

"So this is how you're going to be, is it?" Cud hollered. "Too bad, Mary. If you won't come to us, we'll come to you. Get ready. I'm about to show you what happens to those who make me mad."

20

Fargo was ready. The Henry was wedged to his shoulder, and the hammer was back. His finger was around the trigger.

"Do I shoot, too?" Mary asked.

"You sure as hell do."

Three men rose from concealment and converged on the stand. Howell was the only one Fargo recognized. One of the others was faster and pulled ahead, firing spaced shots. None came anywhere near Fargo or Mary. She started shooting but she missed.

By then Fargo had a perfect bead. He thought of the two times fate had thwarted him and prayed there wouldn't be a third. He stroked the trigger.

Thirty feet out, the outlaw pitched onto his belly. He lost his hat and his rifle and broke into fierce convulsions but they only lasted a few seconds. A screech, and he was no more.

Fargo fed another round into the chamber.

Howell and the other two had turned and were flying back to the forest.

They fired as they ran but they were poor shots when they were moving. Quiet fell.

The dead man had one arm bent under him. Red stained the snow with the essence of death.

"I didn't hit anyone," Mary said.

"Next time."

Oaths blistered the air. Cud Stern could cuss rings around

a mule skinner. "I know you're in there, Fargo. My gal couldn't hit the broad side of a bank if she was standing next to it."

Mary shouted, "Step out in the open and try me. I might surprise you."

"You've surprised me enough as it is. Taking up with another man while I was away. Running out on me. I used to admire you for being a lady but now—" Cud stopped.

"Now you want me dead. All that talk of how much you admired me, when all you really wanted was to get up under my dress." Mary recoiled and put a hand to her cheek. "Oh, my. I did it again. The children will think I'm a hussy."

"You have me all wrong, gal. I figured to make you mine and treat you right. I'd bring you presents now and then, like I brought those cows. Maybe fetch you a new dress. And all you had to do, when the law was breathing down my neck, was let me lie low at your cabin. Yes, sir, I had it all worked out."

"That's all I ever was to you. A convenience. A place to hide and a bed to sleep in."

"Give me more credit. You were all of those but you were more. I never had a real lady before. Only saloon gals."

"You're despicable." Silence fell on the forest.

Fargo wondered what Sten's next move would be. Charging the stand wasn't the answer. Sten had to come up with something else, and he was devious enough to come up with something that might take them unawares.

Mary was staring at Fargo. "I can't tell you how happy I am you came along when you did. You saved me from that pig."

"Not yet I haven't." Fargo didn't take his eyes off the tree line. He looked for patches of color against the white.

"It won't be dark for hours yet," Mary said, squinting up at the sun. "We'll be safe until then, won't we?"

"We won't be safe until Sten is dead."

Mary turned and gazed into the lodgepoles. "Do you mind if I check on Jayce and Nelly? I won't be long. They must be scared, and I need to let them know everything is all right."

"Off you go." Fargo rested his chin on his forearm. He was cold lying there, and he imagined Sten and his killers were cold, too. Extra cause for them to end it quickly.

A hat poked from behind a pine. Fargo aimed but the head wearing the hat ducked back.

"Mary, you still there?" Sten called.

"She's busy," Fargo shouted.

"Ah. The simpleton speaks. What's she doing, cooking your supper?"

Fargo kept the Henry trained on where the head had appeared. All it would take was a twitch of his finger.

"Simpleton?" Cud Sten shouted.

Fargo waited, with no intention of answering.

"Tell me something. What happened to Rika? That was his horse one of you was riding, wasn't it? You were too far off for me to be sure."

"It's his horse," Fargo confirmed.

"He's dead, isn't he? Who was it? You? Had to be. Mary never harmed a soul her whole life. She told me so."

Fargo saw no need to enlighten him.

"You must be good, mister, to have done in Rika. He was one of the best. He hardly ever made a mistake. All the years we rode together, I can count them on one hand and have fingers left over."

Fargo grew suspicious. Sten was talking too much.

"How did you do it, mister? Did you take him by surprise somehow? Did you trick him?"

Movement out of the corner of his eye warned Fargo that Sten's men were trying to flank him. One of them was crawling toward the stand from off to the left. Or maybe burrowing was a better word. The man was digging through the snow like an oversized rodent, and gave himself away when the top of his hat jutted up.

Fargo swiveled and fixed a bead, but the hat had disappeared. He aimed a few feet in front of where he saw it, counted off five seconds to give the man time to reach the spot where he was aiming, and fired. Nothing happened. He levered in another round and fired again.

Up bolted Howell. With remarkable speed he raced back toward the forest, weaving so it would be harder to hit him.

Fargo watched Howell's legs and nothing else, and when they zagged where he expected them to, he stroked the trigger and had the satisfaction of hearing Howell yelp in pain and seeing him fall. But in another instant Howell was up and leaping like mad on one leg. Fargo fixed another bead, but before he could shoot, Howell gained cover.

Cud Sten wasn't pleased. "Damn it, Howell. Can't you do anything right? Did you have to go and get shot?"

From behind the tree Howell had dived behind came his pain-laced reply. "I tried, didn't I? Just as you wanted. And now I've got a hole in me."

"How bad is it?"

"I can still do what I have to, if that's what you're worried about. The bullet went clean through and it's not bleeding much."

"We'll bandage you when we're done here."

Fargo congratulated himself. Sten had kept him talking so that Howell could sneak up on him, and he had spoiled their little scheme. Then it occurred to him that they were much too casual about it, especially Sten.

"A man just can't find good help these days," Cud shouted across to him. "That's why I miss Rika so much."

Fargo sought some sign of the other two. They had to be there somewhere.

"I've got my club with me," Cud gabbed on. "Remember

my club, mister? You'll remember it real well when I start breaking bones."

One of the others showed himself for a split second when he darted from one tree to another.

Now Fargo had accounted for three of them. But where was the fourth?

"I like to break bones. I like to hear them snap, hear the crack of an arm or the pop of an elbow. Knees now—they sort of crunch. Some say the knees hurt the worst, and I believe it. You should hear how they carry on. A woman one time, I broke one of her knees, just one, and she shrieked and flopped about like a fish out of water for a good hour or more. Then there was the old man I did once. I hanged him by his wrists from a tree and started at his toes and worked up his body. And do you know what? He didn't scream until I got to his knees."

Fargo was puzzled by why Sten was telling him all this. He was puzzled, too, that Mary was taking so long. He twisted around, and there they were: Mary and Nelly and Jayce, the children pressed to her in fear. Behind them, holding a revolver to Mary's head, was Lear.

"I'd let go of that rifle if I were you, mister. Or would your rather have me splatter her brains?"

Mary said quickly, "Don't do it, Skye. Not on my account."

Fargo set the Henry down and it sank an inch into the snow. He slowly elevated his hands.

Lear chortled. "That was right noble of you. I wouldn't have done it, but then I don't give a good damn about anybody but me." He tilted his head. "Cud! It worked! I've got them covered! Get over here!"

"I'm sorry," Mary said to Fargo. "He snuck up on us. I was going to shout to warn you, but he said he'd shoot Nelly and Jayce if I didn't do exactly as he told me."

"Shut up," Lear barked, and rapped her above the ear.

Mary cried out and nearly collapsed. She stared to raise a hand to her head, and he hit her on the elbow.

"Did I say you can move?"

Tears welled in Jayce's eyes. He balled his fists and shook one at Lear. "Leave my ma be!"

"Or what, boy? You'll cry me to death?"

Nelly gripped her brother's shoulders to keep him from hurling himself at Lear. "No, Jayce. He'll hurt us if we do anything."

"That I will, girl. At least one of you has brains." Lear grinned. He was relishing the torment he caused.

Feet crunched in the snow.

"At last it has gone my way," Cud Sten said. After him came Howell, who was limping, and the last outlaw.

"It was easy as could be," Lear boasted.

Cud had a revolver in one hand and his club in the other. He shoved the club nearly in Fargo's face, saying, "Scared yet? You should be. The breaking is about to begin."

Fargo was amazed at how careless they were. Not one had demanded he shed his Colt. But then, he was partly on his side, propped on an elbow, his holster hidden by his arm.

Mary suddenly stepped close to Cud. Lear went to strike her, but Cud shook his head and Lear reluctantly lowered his revolver.

"I have a proposition for you. It involves him." Mary pointed at Fargo. "Let him live and I'll agree to be your woman. I'll do whatever you want me to do."

"Bitch," Cud said.

"You've wanted me for a long time, haven't you? I'm yours. All you have to do is let him get on his horse and ride off."

"Is that all?" Cud made as if to strike her, himself. "You rub my nose in it, gal. You offer yourself for him. And you expect me to let him waltz away?"

All eyes were on Sten and Mary.

Fargo slowly sat up, careful to keep his holster hidden. He propped his hand on the ground and went to rise, but a rifle was pointed at his chest.

"Stay right where you are, mister," Howell warned.

"Whatever you say." Fargo shrugged and started to sink back down. In reality, he was girding himself, and when Howell glanced at Sten and Mary, he exploded into motion. Drawing as he rose, Fargo fired from the hip and shot Howell smack between the eyes. He swiveled and put lead into the chest of the outlaw whose name he didn't know. He swiveled again, saw Lear jerk his rifle, and fanned two swift shots that jolted Lear off his feet.

That left Cud Sten.

Fargo swiveled toward him—just as a streak of brown slammed against his gun hand, knocking the Colt from his grasp. He lunged for it but the club was faster. His entire arm flared with searing pain. He tried to grab the club with his other hand, only to have Cud Sten step in close and club him over the head. Snow rushed up to meet his face, and for a few seconds, he was too dazed to move. A hand gripped the back of his shirt and roughly flipped him over.

"God, I'm going to enjoy this," Sten said.

"No!" Mary cried, and threw herself at Cud Sten. He backhanded her with the club, and down she went.

"Ma!" Jayce leaped at Sten, Nelly a step behind him.

Cud clubbed them both. "Damn gnats," he growled. Then, looming over Fargo, he raised the club on high. "Don't worry. I didn't kill them. I aim to have fun with them first. After I'm done with you."

Fargo tried to push to his feet, but he couldn't make his body do what he wanted. A blow to the shoulder flattened him. Another rendered his legs next to useless. Again he was grabbed and turned.

"I'm just getting started," Sten said.

Fargo got an arm up to protect himself but it did no good.

The club connected with his wrist, with his ribs, with his hip. Through a haze of pain, he watched Cud raise the club overhead for the most brutal blow yet. And a strange thing happened. Cud's left eye sprouted feathers. A second later his right eye did the same. Cud's mouth opened and he tottered back, tripped, and keeled onto his back. He twitched once, and would never twitch again.

Fargo turned his head.

There were three of them: the old Indian he had shared his pemmican with and two young warriors. The younger ones held bows. The old Indian looked at Fargo with kindly eyes and smiled. Then he said something and the three of them turned and walked off, just like that.

It took every ounce of will Fargo possessed, but he made it to his hands and knees and over to the Harpers. All three had bumps on their heads, but they would live. Mary was already coming around, and he helped her to sit up.

"What happened?"

Fargo stared at the arrows sticking out of Cud Sten's face. "Three pieces of pemmican saved our lives."

The Black Hills, 1861—woe to the white man who
invaded the land of the Lakotas.

It was like looking for a pink needle in a green-and-brown
haystack.

Or so Skye Fargo thought as he scanned the prairie for the
girl. She would be easy to spot if it weren't for the fact there
was so *much* prairie. A sea of grass stretched from Canada to
Mexico, broken here and there by rivers and mountain ranges.

North of him, not yet in sight, were the Black Hills.

Fargo didn't like being there. He was in Sioux country,
and the Sioux were not fond of whites these days. More often than not, any white they came across was treated to a
quiver of arrows or had his throat slit and his hair lifted so it
could hang from a coup stick in a warrior's lodge.

Fargo was white but it was hard to tell by looking at him.
His skin was bronzed dark by the relentless sun. He had lake

blue eyes, something no Sioux ever had. He wore buckskins. A white hat, a red bandanna, and boots were the rest of his attire. A Colt with well-worn grips was strapped around his waist. In an ankle sheath nestled an Arkansas toothpick. From his saddle scabbard jutted the stock of a Henry rifle.

Rising in the stirrups, Fargo squinted against the glare of the sun and raked the grass from east to west and back again. It wasn't flat, not this close to the Hills. A maze of gullies and washes made spotting her that much harder.

"Damn all kids, anyhow," Fargo grumbled out loud. He gigged the Ovaro and rode on, vowing that there would be hell to pay when he got back to the party he was guiding.

A shrill whistle drew his gaze to a prairie dog. It had spotted him and was warning its friends.

Fargo swung wide of the prairie dog town. The last thing he needed was for the Ovaro to step into a hole and break a leg. He intended to keep the stallion a good long while. It was the best horse he had ever ridden. Often, it meant the difference between his breathing air or dirt.

"Where could she have gotten to?"

Fargo had a habit of talking to himself. It came from being alone so much. He was a frontiersman or, as some would call him, a plainsman, although he spent as much time in the mountains as he did roaming the grasslands. Wide spaces, empty of people, were what he liked it.

He came to the crest of a knoll and drew rein again. Twisting from side to side, he still couldn't spot her. Frowning, he indulged in a few choice cuss words. He began to regret ever taking this job.

About to ride on, Fargo glanced down, and froze. Hoofprints showed he wasn't the first on that knoll. The tracks were made by unshod horses, which meant Indians, and in this instance undoubtedly meant Sioux. There had been five of them.

They had passed that way several days ago. That was good. They were long gone and posed no danger to the girl.

There was a lot of other danger: Bears, wolves, cougars, and rattlesnakes called the prairie home. Most times they left people alone, but not always, and it was the not always that worried him. To a griz the girl would be no more than a snack. A hungry wolf might decide to try something new. As for cougars, they'd kill and eat just about anything they could catch.

"The ornery brat," Fargo groused some more. He kept riding and was soon amid a maze of coulees.

Fargo could see the headlines now. *Senator's Daughter Ripped Apart by Wild Beast!* Or *Hunting Trip Ends in Tragedy.* Or *Famous Trailsman Loses Child to Meat Eater.* That last one was the likeliest. Journalists loved to write about him, often making stories up out of whole cloth. The more sensational the tale, the better. All to boost circulation. Were it up to him, he'd take every scribbler alive and throw them down a well.

Fargo rounded a bend and drew rein. In the grass ahead lay something yellow and pink. Suspecting what it was, he dismounted and walked over, his spurs jingling. The girl's doll grinned up at him. He picked it up. The blond curls and pink dress were a copy of the girl and the dress she often wore.

She had been there and dropped the doll. That worried him. She never went anywhere without the thing. She even slept with it. She wouldn't run off and leave it.

A scream split the air.

Fargo was in the saddle before it died. He reined sharply in the direction the scream came from. Half a minute of hard riding and he found her at last. She wasn't alone.

Gertrude Keever had her back to a dirt bank and was kicking at the creatures trying to sink their teeth into her.

There were two of them: coyotes. Ordinarily their kind stayed well shy of humans, but this pair was scrawny. Either they were sickly or poor hunters, and they were hungry enough to go after Gerty.

Fargo drew his Colt and fired into the ground. He had nothing against the coyotes. They were only trying to fill their bellies. At the blast, one of them ran off. The other didn't even look up. It kept on snapping at the girl's legs and missed by a whisker.

"Kill this stupid thing, you simpleton!" the girl yelled.

Fargo almost wished the coyote had bitten her. He fired from the hip and cored its head.

Gerty glared at him. "Took you long enough." She stepped to the dead coyote, squatted, and stuck a finger in the bullet hole. The she held her finger up and grinned as she watched the blood trickle down.

"What the hell are you doing?" Fargo asked.

The girl held her finger higher for him to see. "Look. Isn't it pretty?"

Swinging down, Fargo walked over, gripped her elbow, and jerked her to her feet. "You damn nuisance. Wash your face with it, why don't you?"

"I'm going to tell Father on you. He won't like how you talk to me. He won't like it one bit."

Fargo sighed. For a thirteen-year-old, she was as big a bitch as some women three times her age. "I'll do more than talk if you don't start showing some common sense."

"What do you mean?"

Fargo nodded at the dead coyote. "What the hell do you think I mean? You nearly got eaten. You can't go wandering off whenever you want. It's too damn dangerous."

"Oh, bosh. You've been saying that since the first day, and nothing has happened."

Fargo didn't point out that nothing happened because he made it a point to keep them safe. Instead, he shook her, hard. "You'll do as you're supposed to, or I'll take you over my knee."

"You wouldn't!"

"Don't try me." Fargo hauled her to the Ovaro. He had put up with her shenanigans because her father was paying him, but there were limits to how much he'd abide.

Fargo had never met a girl like her. Gerty looked so sweet and innocent with her wide green eyes and golden curls, but she had a heart of pure evil. She was constantly killing things. Bugs, mostly, since they were about all she could catch. Although once, near the Platte, they had come on a baby bird that had fallen from its nest, and Gerty beaned it with a rock. Her father thought it was hilarious.

Not Fargo. He had seen her pulls wings from butterflies and moths, throw ants into the fire, and try to gouge out her pony's eyes when it didn't do what she wanted. He'd never met a child like her.

"What are you doing?" Gerty demanded.

"Taking you back," Fargo said.

Gerty stamped her foot. "I don't want to go back. I want to explore some more."

"Didn't that coyote teach you anything?" Fargo swung her onto the saddle and climbed on behind her. "Hold on to the horn."

"The what?"

"That thing sticking up in front of you." Fargo tapped his spurs and went up the side of the coulee, making a beeline for camp. The summer sun was warm on his face, the scent of grass strong.

Gerty swiveled her head to fix him with another glare. "I don't like you. I don't like you an awful lot."

"Good for you."

"My so-called mother does, though."

"She said that?" Fargo liked the senator's wife. She was quiet and polite, and she always spoke kindly to him. She also had the kind of body that made men drool.

"Forget about her. It's me who can't stand your guts."

"As if I give a damn." Fargo was alert for sign of the Sioux. Venturing into their territory was never the brightest of notions. But the senator had insisted on hunting in the notorious Black Hills.

"In fact, I'm starting to hate you."

"I'm sure I'll lose sleep over it."

Gerty was fit to burst her boiler. She flushed red with fury. "Don't you want to know why?"

"No."

"I'll tell you anyway. You're mean. You stopped me from poking my pony with that stick. You wouldn't let me kill that frog by the Platte River. And when I killed that baby bird, you called me a jackass. Father didn't hear you, but I did, as plain as day."

"You have good ears."

Gerty cocked her arm to punch him.

"I wouldn't," Fargo advised. "I hit a lot harder than you do."

"You wouldn't dare. Father would be mad. He won't pay you the rest of your money."

"Then I'll hit him."

Gerty laughed. "You don't know anything. Father is an important man. You hit him and he'll have you arrested."

Fargo motioned at the unending vista of prairie. "Do you see a tin star anywhere?" To his relief she shut up, but she simmered like a pot put on to boil. She was so used to getting her own way that when someone had the gall to stand up to her, she hated it.

Her father was to blame. Senator Fulton Keever was a big man in Washington, D.C. The senior senator from New York, Keever had made a name for himself standing up for what the newspapers called "the little people." He was also reputed to be something of a hunter and had the distinction of bagging the biggest black bear ever shot in that state.

"What are those?" Gerty asked, pointing.

Fargo wanted to kick himself. He'd let his attention wander. He looked and felt his pulse quicken. Four riders were silhouetted against the western horizon. They were too far off to note much detail but there could be no mistake: They were Sioux warriors. A hunting part, most likely, but they wouldn't hesitate to kill any whites they came across.

Fargo had to find cover before they spotted the Ovaro. A buffalo wallow was handy, and he reined down into it.

"Land sakes." Gerty covered her mouth and nose and asked through her fingers, "What's that awful stink?"

"Buffalo piss."

"What?"

"Buffalo like to roll in the dirt. Sometimes they pee in it and get mud all over them to keep off the flies and whatnot."

"It smells terrible. Get me out of here this instant."

"We're not going anywhere just yet." Not until Fargo was good and sure the warriors were gone.

Twisting, Gerty poked him in the chest. "My father will hear of this. I'll tell him all about how you've treated me."

"That threat is getting old."

"You're a despicable person—do you know that?"

There had been times, admittedly few, when Fargo wondered what it would be like to have a wife and kids. He made a mental note that the next time he began to wonder, he'd think of Gerty. She was enough to make any man swear off kids for life.

"Why don't you say something?" Gerty said. "How can you stand the odor?"

"Quit flapping your gums and hold your breath and it won't be as bad." None of the buffalo tracks, Fargo saw, were fresh, which was just as well. It wouldn't do to have a buff come along and take exception to their being there.

"Have I mentioned I'm starting to hate you?"

"Have I mentioned I don't give a damn?"

"I hope a rattlesnake bites you."

Fargo was commencing to regret ever agreeing to guide the Keevers. The senator was paying him almost twice what most guide jobs earned, but the money wasn't enough for what Fargo had to put up with.

Fargo had been in Denver, gambling, when an older gentleman in a suit and bowler looked him up and asked if he would be so kind as to pay Senator Fulton Keever a visit at the Imperial. Fargo was on a losing streak anyway, so he went.

Keever had welcomed him warmly. It turned out the senator was on a hunting trip and needed a guide. Keever had heard Fargo was in town and sought him out. Fargo wasn't all that interested until Keever mentioned how much he was willing to pay.

"I have a question, you lump of clay," Gerty said, interrupting Fargo's musing.

"Hush, girl." Fargo was tired of her jabber.

"It's important."

"I doubt that."

"Are buffalo friendly?"

"About as friendly as you are."

"That one over there doesn't look very friendly." Gerty pointed up at the rim.

Silhouetted against the sun was a bull buffalo.